# Annabelle sighed. "What are you doing here?"

He wished he knew. It had seemed so simple when his mother had suggested it. Help get Annie out of town. But being around her messed with more than his mind. "I'm going to help you pack up the house and take what you don't want to the dump—unless you want to argue about that, too?"

"I know you think I'm a charity case that you have to—"

"You never were graceful when it came to taking help from anyone," he interrupted. "Just say thank you and let's leave it at that."

She clamped her jaw shut for a moment. "I'm also not graceful when people pity me."

He let out a bark of a laugh. "You think that's what this is? Sorry, sister, but you are the last person I feel sorry for. You need to get your grandmother's house ready to sell. You want to sell this house and clear out of town? Fine with me. I had some things to take to the dump. I thought I'd take some of yours." He gave her a challenging look. "But if you don't want my help—"

# HARD RUSTLER

New York Times Bestselling Author
## B.J. DANIELS

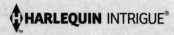

This book is for Julie Simundson Nagy, a true fan, who has been a bright spot in so many of my days. Writing is such a solitary endeavor with lots of stress. I will see Julie and she will remind me that I'm not alone in this. Her smile and enthusiasm keep me grounded. Thank you, Julie!

ISBN-13: 978-1-335-52658-8

Hard Rustler

Copyright © 2018 by Barbara Heinlein

Recycling programs
for this product may
not exist in your area.

This edition published by arrangement with Harlequin Books S.A.

For questions and comments about the quality of this book, please contact us at CustomerService@Harlequin.com.

Printed in U.S.A.

www.Harlequin.com

**B.J. Daniels** is a *New York Times* and *USA TODAY* bestselling author. She wrote her first book after a career as an award-winning newspaper journalist and author of thirty-seven published short stories. She lives in Montana with her husband, Parker, and three springer spaniels. When not writing, she quilts, boats and plays tennis. Contact her at bjdaniels.com, on Facebook or on Twitter, @bjdanielsauthor.

### Books by B.J. Daniels

#### Harlequin Intrigue

##### Whitehorse, Montana: The Clementine Sisters

*Hard Rustler*

##### The Montana Cahills

*Cowboy's Redemption*

##### Whitehorse, Montana: The McGraw Kidnapping

*Dark Horse*
*Dead Ringer*
*Rough Rider*

#### HQN Books

##### The Montana Cahills

*Renegade's Pride*
*Outlaw's Honor*
*Hero's Return*
*Rancher's Dream*

Visit the Author Profile page at Harlequin.com.

## CAST OF CHARACTERS

**_Dawson Rogers_**—The rancher had lost the love of his life because he was never leaving Montana and the life he loved.

**_Annabelle Clementine_**—She'd followed her dream and it had cost her dearly. Now desperate, the former supermodel was back in Whitehorse, Montana, only to sell her deceased grandmother's house.

**_Grandma Francesca Clementine_**—She'd raised her three granddaughters to be free spirits. Little did they know what a free spirit she'd been in her younger days. But the secret was in the house—soon to be uncovered.

**_Bernard "Bernie the Hawk" McDougal_**—Before he died, the old Irish mobster was determined to find the woman he loved—and the loot she'd stolen from him all those years ago.

**_Mary Sue Linton_**—The Realtor loved a good mystery. Why anyone would wall up a perfectly good alcove was definitely a head-scratcher.

**_Wilhelmina Rogers_**—She would never stoop to matchmaking to get her oldest son together with the woman he loved. Unless she thought it might work.

**_Lawrence Clarkston_**—He had his own reasons for wanting to get into Frannie Clementine's house.

**_Inez Gilbert_**—The nosy neighbor saw enough to be suspicious.

**_Saddie_**—Even the dog knew something was amiss in Frannie's house.

# Chapter One

As her sports car topped the rise, Annabelle Clementine looked out at the rugged country spread before her and felt her heart drop. She'd never thought she'd see so many miles of wild winter Montana landscape ever again. At least, she'd hoped not.

How could she have forgotten the remoteness? The vastness? The isolation? There wasn't a town in sight. Or a ranch house. Or another living soul.

She glanced down at her gas gauge. It hovered at empty. She'd tried to get gas at the last station, but her credit card wouldn't work and she'd gone through almost all of her cash. She'd put in what fuel she could with the change she was able scrape up, but it had barely moved the gauge. If she ran out of gas before she reached Whitehorse…well, it would just be her luck, wouldn't it?

She let the expensive silver sports car coast down the mountain toward the deep gorge of the Missouri River, thankful that most of the snow was high in the mountains and not on the highway. She didn't know what she would have done if the roads had been icy since she hadn't seen a snow tire since she'd left Montana.

The motor coughed. She looked down at the gauge. The engine had to be running on fumes. What was she going to do? It was still miles to Whitehorse. Tears burned her eyes, but she refused to cry. Yes, things were bad. Really bad. But—

She was almost to the river bottom when she saw it. At a wide spot where the river wound on its way through Montana east to the Mississippi, a pickup and horse trailer were pulled off to the side of the highway. Her pulse jumped at just the thought of another human being—let alone the possibility of getting some fuel. If she could just get to Whitehorse…

But as she descended the mountain, she didn't see anyone around the pickup or horse trailer. What if the rig had been left beside the road and the driver was nowhere to be found? Maybe there would be a gas can in the back of the pickup or—*Have you stooped so low that now you would steal gas?*

Fortunately, she wasn't forced to answer that. She spotted a cowboy standing on the far side of the truck. Her instant of relief was quickly doused as she looked around and realized how alone the two of them were, out here in the middle of nowhere.

*Don't be silly. What are the chances the cowboy is a serial killer, rapist, kidnapper, ax murderer…?* The motor sputtered as if taking its last gasp as she slowed. It wasn't as if she had a choice. She hadn't seen another car for over an hour. For miles she'd driven through open country dotted occasionally with cows but no people. And she knew there was nothing but rugged country the rest of the way north to Whitehorse.

If there had been any other way to get where she was headed, she would have taken it. But her options had been limited for some time now.

And today, it seemed, her options had come down to this cowboy and possible serial killer rapist kidnapper ax murderer.

She let the car glide into the spot next to where the cowboy had pulled off the highway. *I'll just bum a little fuel and be on my way. Nothing to worry about.* Just the thought made her laugh. Her life was one big worry right now, she fretted, as she took in the rangy-looking cowboy standing by his truck.

"What's the worst that could happen?" She groaned. *Taking risks is what got you into this mess.* Like she had to be reminded.

The engine let out a final cough and died. Committed now, she had no choice as she braked next to the horse trailer. Turning off the key in the ignition, she checked her makeup and hair in the mirror. *You're Annabelle Clementine. You can do this.* The woman who stared back at her from the mirror looked skeptical at best.

Bucking up her courage, she stepped out of the car, careful not to let her last pair of expensive heels get muddy. "Excuse me?" she called, determined also not to get too far away from her open car door. "I'm afraid I have a small problem and really could use some help."

She was ready to make a hasty retreat back into the car, if need be. Not that she would be going far if things went south. But at least she could lock herself in. She instantly regretted the fact that she'd bought a canvas-topped convertible, which had been perfect in Southern California.

The cowboy had his back to her and hadn't looked up from where he'd been digging around in the back of his pickup bed.

"Excuse me?" she tried again. He had to have heard her. But so far, he hadn't acknowledged her presence in any way.

Forced to move away from the car, she took in the cowboy as she approached and wasn't impressed with what she saw. But then again, she'd grown up with cowboys so she'd never understood the fascination. Admittedly, this one was tall, broad shouldered, slim hipped, long legged and not bad from the backside.

Unfortunately, everything else about him looked worn and dirty, from his jeans, boots and canvas jacket to the Stetson on the too-long dark hair curling at the nape of his red neck.

At her approach, he gave her a quick glance over his shoulder. She could see little of his face. He wore mirrored sunglasses against the winter glare, his hat pulled low. Under the dark shadow of his Stetson, she glimpsed several week's growth of beard, making him look even more craggy and unkempt. No designer stubble on this cowboy.

Either he'd been on the range for days or this was as good as it got with him.

*You're not marrying him. You're just bumming fuel.* "Hello?" she said louder and with more attitude as he went back to what he was doing.

"There a problem?" he drawled in a low, lazy tone as he finally finished and turned, seemingly reluctantly, to give her his attention. She saw that he'd been feeding his dog in the back of the pickup. The dog—little more than a puppy—was a furry mutt with one blue eye and one brown one circled by a patch of black. He didn't look much better than his owner.

She shifted her gaze back to the cowboy who was looking at her car as if he'd never seen one like it before. *Probably doesn't get off the ranch much.*

He slowly slid his gaze back to her with a nonchalance that made her grind her teeth.

"Yes, there is a problem." She'd thought she'd already told him that.

He lifted the brim of his hat, dropped his sunglasses down to look over them for a moment. She caught a glimpse of brown eyes as he surveyed her, making her feel nearly naked under the black cashmere sweater and slacks she was wearing, before he lifted his sunglasses again.

"I'm afraid I forgot to buy gas at the last station," she said, wanting to get this over with as quickly as possible—even if it did make her look like a fool. She had worse problems. "I was wondering if you might have some gas that I could borrow? Just enough to get me into town?"

*"Borrow?"* He chuckled at that. "And town being?"

She hated to even admit where she was headed. "Whitehorse."

"That's another hour up the road."

As if she didn't know that. "My car used more gas

than I thought it would." She gave a nervous laugh, hating that she had to resort to acting as if she didn't have a brain. Back when she was making money, fuel was never an issue. She hadn't realized how much a lot of things cost—until she couldn't pay for them anymore.

He nodded, glancing toward the river as if considering her request. "I suppose I could siphon some out of one of my tanks." He didn't sound thrilled about it. Nor had he moved.

"I would appreciate that so much." She glanced at her watch.

"Got some place to be, do you?"

"I have an appointment."

"In Whitehorse?" From under the brim of his hat and behind the mirrored sunglasses, he studied her a few moments more before he sighed. "Best pull up next to my pickup while I grab a hose."

She feared the car wouldn't start, let alone move. But there must have been just enough fumes left for her to pull up before it died again. She shut off the engine, staying in the car to pop the gas compartment open and watch him move slow as molasses. He acted as if he had all day. *He* probably did.

Patience had never been one of her strong suits. She tapped a toe as she heard him talking to his dog, mumbling so she couldn't make out a word. As if she didn't know he was giving the dog an earful about her.

The dog, still in the pickup bed, wagged its tail enthusiastically at whatever the cowboy said. Whatever he was saying, he certainly found it amusing from that hint of a grin under the beard. Annabelle consoled herself with the thought that the mutt was probably the closest thing the cowboy could get to a female companion.

After a good five to ten minutes, he finished. She hadn't thought past getting enough gas to get to Whitehorse. Now her stomach clenched at a thought. Not only should she offer him money, but he also might demand it. And since she had no money and doubted he took credit cards—even ones that weren't frozen for lack of payment...

She watched him walk to his pickup to put the hose away and knew what she had to do. It was the coward's way out. But she told herself that she had no choice. She'd been telling herself that for months now. Not that it made her feel any better as she quickly started her car and threw it into reverse.

Whirring down the passenger side window, she called out, "Thank you so much. If you're ever in Whitehorse..." With that she took off, torn between guilt and glee over seeing that he'd given her almost a full tank of gas.

When she dared look back, she saw him standing by his pickup shaking his head as he watched her leave. She thought of that glimpse of golden brown. Even shaded under the brim of his old Stetson, those eyes... They'd almost seemed...familiar.

## Chapter Two

Dawson Rogers swore as he pulled off his worn Stetson. Raking a hand through his hair, he watched the silver sports car take off like a bat out of hell.

"Annabelle Clementine." He said the name like a curse. For years, he'd only seen her staring back at him from glossy women's magazine ads. He'd been just fine knowing there was no chance that he'd ever lay eyes on her in the flesh again. She'd been real clear about never setting foot in this state again when she'd left all those years ago.

So what was she doing headed for Whitehorse?

That his heart was still pounding only made him more furious with himself. When he'd heard her voice behind him…he couldn't believe it. He'd thought for sure that his worn-out, dog-weary body was playing tricks on him. He'd frozen in place, counting to ten and then ten again, afraid to turn around for fear he'd be wrong—or worse—right.

Now he swore, remembering his reaction to just the sound of her voice. Could he be a bigger fool?

And yet that voice had brought it all back. The ache

in his belly, the stompin' she'd done on his heart. Worse, the hope that set a fire inside him at just the sound of it. In that instant, he'd wanted it to be her more than he'd wanted his next breath. After everything she'd done to him, he'd actually felt a spike of joy at the thought of seeing her again.

And still he hadn't turned around, because he'd known once he did, the disappointment would be as painful as the last time he'd seen her.

Turning, he'd seen her standing there and thought, *Damn, the woman is even more beautiful than when she'd hightailed it out of here.*

He'd been shocked—and still was. Annie. In the flesh. That she hadn't changed except to become more gorgeous had left him shaken. A dust devil of emotions whirled inside him as he watched her drive away.

"What is she doing back here?" he demanded as the pup came over to the side of the pickup bed to lick his hand.

Sadie wagged her tail in response. "What am I doing asking you?" He ruffled the dog's fur. Still, he found himself squinting after the sports car as it climbed the mountain on the other side of the river and disappeared around a curve. "What's a woman who said she'd never set foot in Whitehorse doing back here? If I hadn't seen her with my own eyes…"

For just a moment there, earlier, before she'd asked for gas, he'd thought…

Hell, he didn't want to think about what he'd thought as he shoved his hat back on. "Let's get on home," he said to the pup as he reminded himself that Annabelle Clementine's coming back had nothing to do with him.

He told himself that he shouldn't have been surprised that she hadn't changed. Still, it galled him. Her clothes might be more expensive and she drove a much fancier car, but she was still the same girl who'd looked down her nose at him—and Whitehorse—all those years ago.

It nagged at him. What could have brought her back? He shook his head, telling himself it was obviously none of his business. Best thing he could do was to forget about her—something he'd been working on for some time now.

After two weeks in hunting camp, he recalled that before he'd seen her, all he'd wanted was to get home, have a hot shower and climb into a warm, soft bed. If he hadn't stopped beside the road to take a leak, let Sadie out and give the pup a snack…well, he might not have seen her at all.

The only thing that didn't surprise him, he told himself as he lifted Sadie into the pickup's front seat and climbed behind the wheel, was that the woman hadn't given him the time of day. Hell, he couldn't even be sure she remembered him. After all, it had been… How many years *had* it been? He wondered with a frown as he started the truck engine.

Thirteen. He let out a low whistle. Sadie's ears perked up, but she lay back down and closed her eyes for the ride home.

And it wasn't like Annie had ever given him a thought since she'd been gone, he reminded himself. She'd made it perfectly clear that they had no future before she'd left right after high school to find fame and fortune.

Dawson pointed the pickup toward Whitehorse, all the time trying to imagine what could have brought her back. Certainly not her grandmother's funeral. Only her two sisters had made it back for that. Of course, they'd attended the funeral and left right away, but at least they'd shown up. He shook his head, thinking that he'd expected better of the girl he'd fallen in love with all those years ago. Given how much her grandmother had doted on her...

But he reminded himself that he'd *always* been wrong about the woman. He could no more predict what Annabelle was going to do than predict the Montana weather. He thought of that young fool cowboy who'd saved every dime he made that year to promise her something that would make her stay. He growled under his breath at the memory.

Well, he wasn't that young fool anymore. Which was why he was going to give her a wide berth as long as she was in town. Not that he suspected it would be for long. Knowing her, she would be hightailing it back to California as fast as she could. Back to her fancy life in the spotlight.

"Which is just fine with us, huh, Sadie," he said to his pup. "Don't need the likes of her around here messing with our minds." Sadie barked in answer and curled closer to him, making him laugh. "This was before your time," he said to the dog, "But that woman was once nothing but walking heartache for this cowboy. Fortunately, I'm not that man anymore."

His words sounded hollow, even to him. He felt his face flush at how much gas he'd given her and mentally kicked himself. He should have left her beside the road to fend for herself. But then, he'd never been able to say no to her—even when he should have known that a girl like her wanted something better than a cowboy like him.

ANNABELLE PUT THE cowboy and his dog behind her as she drove north. She was determined that nothing would get in her way. Once she did what she'd come for, she was out of here. Another one of those limited options.

She took the back way into the small Western town. The first settlement of Whitehorse had been nearer the Missouri River. But when the railroad came through, the town migrated north, taking the name with it. Old Town Whitehorse, as it was now known, was little more than a ghost town to the south.

Not that Whitehorse proper was a thriving metropolis. The whole town was only ten blocks square. Nothing but a siding along the railroad tracks more than a hundred years ago, it had become a small rural town like a lot of small rural Montana towns.

Why her grandmother had settled here was still a mystery, but when Annabelle's parents had been killed, Grandma Frannie had taken Annabelle and her two sisters in without hesitation. Annabelle had grown up here, dreaming of a life she envisioned far from this dusty old Western town.

As she drove down the tree-lined street with the large houses that backed onto the Milk River, images of her childhood flickered like the winter sun coming through the leafless cottonwood trees. From as far back as she could remember, she'd grown up with one thing in mind: getting out of this town and making something of her life.

That sick feeling she'd become acquainted with over the past few months now settled in her stomach. Right now, she couldn't face even thinking about how she'd messed up. Sitting up a little straighter behind the wheel of the car, she assured herself that everything was going to be fine.

She would just take care of business and put all the unpleasantness behind her. As she tried to look for a silver lining in all this, she noticed that she still had plenty of gas. It should last her for what little time she would be here, thanks to that cowboy. She shoved away the guilt. If she ever saw him again…

Down the block, she spotted the house. Her foot came off the gas pedal, the car slowing as she felt a rush of déjà vu. The house hadn't changed—just like she doubted the town had—and for a moment it was as if she'd never left. So much had happened to her, she'd expected this part of her past would have changed, somehow.

Instead, it looked so much the same, she almost expected Frannie to come out on the porch as Annabelle pulled up in front of the large, two-story house and shut off the engine. The key to the front door was in her pocket, but she wasn't ready to go inside. Not yet. Glancing at her watch, she saw that she'd gotten here early. There was no sign of the Realtor. Taking a breath, she let it out and tried to relax as she studied the house.

The white siding could use an overall paint job and the emerald trim needed a touch-up. But if she closed her eyes, she could picture herself and her sisters, the three Clementine girls, on that wide porch drinking Grandma Frannie's lemonade and giggling like the schoolgirls they'd been.

She hadn't realized that she'd closed her eyes until she felt them burn with tears. Her guilt was like one of her grandmother's knitting needles to her heart. Yes, she should have made it to Frannie's funeral. She'd had her reasons, and they hadn't all been out of embarrassment for the way her life had turned out.

Her grandmother would have understood because Annabelle had always been the favorite. At least, that's what she told herself.

"You're so much like me, Annabelle Clementine, that sometimes I swear you'll be the death of me." Then Grandma Frannie's expression would soften and she'd press a cool palm to Annabelle's cheek. "So much like me. It's like seeing myself at your age."

"That's why I'm your favorite," she'd say, and her grandmother would shake her head and laugh before telling her to run along outside.

But it had to have been true. Otherwise, why would Frannie have left her the only thing she had of any value—this house. And left it only to her instead of to all three sisters?

A tap on the passenger-side window startled her. Her

eyes flew open, but it took a moment to chase away the bittersweet memories along with the guilt and the tears.

REALTOR MARY SUE Linton glanced at the silver sports car and shook her head. Leave it to Annabelle to show up in something like that. She shouldn't have been surprised since this was the Annabelle Clementine she'd known since grade school.

She had been surprised, though, when her former classmate had called and asked Mary Sue to represent her in the sale. Not surprised. Shocked. The two of them had never been friends, traveling in a completely different circle of friends, even as small as the classes had been. The truth was that Annabelle hadn't uttered two words to her throughout four years of high school. Did people still say stuck-up?

Blonde and blue-eyed, with a figure that Mary Sue would have killed for, Annabelle was The Girl Most Likely to Become Famous. At least, that's what it had said in their senior class yearbook. Everyone knew Annabelle was going to be somebody. Annabelle had said it enough times.

But, then again, she'd also said that she would never come back to Whitehorse. And here she was.

Still, why come all this way to sell her grandmother's house? Mary Sue had told her on the phone that she could deal with everything but the paperwork and save her the trip. She had expected Annabelle to jump at it. Instead, the woman had insisted on coming back to "handle" things.

"If you don't trust me to get you the best price…" Mary Sue had started to say, "you can kiss my—"

But Annabelle had interrupted with, "It's *my* grand-mother's house."

Right. Just like it had been *her* grandmother's funeral. Everyone in town had turned out. Annabelle's two sisters had flown in and out. No Annabelle, though. So was Mary Sue supposed to believe the house had sentimental value to this woman? Not likely.

After tapping on the sports car window, she bent down and looked in. One glance and it was clear that her former classmate had aged well. She looked better than she had in high school. Mary Sue felt that old stab of jealousy.

She started to tap again, but to her surprise, Annabelle appeared to be furtively wiping away tears. Shocked at such a sign of emotion, Mary Sue was taken aback. Maybe she was wrong about Annabelle. Maybe she did have a heart. Maybe she did care about her grandmother. Maybe she even cared about this house and Whitehorse and the people she'd once snubbed.

The thought almost made her laugh though as her former classmate climbed out of the convertible sports car saying, "Okay, let's get this over with so I can get out of this one-horse town."

DAWSON UNLOADED THE horse trailer, parked it and went into the ranch house he'd built himself. He'd worked hard the past thirteen years and now had a place he was proud of on the family ranch. The oldest son of two, he'd had to take over helping his mother run the ranch after his father had died. He'd worked hard and was proud of what he'd been able to accomplish. Annabelle wasn't the only one who'd done well over the years, he told himself with no small amount of defensiveness.

"Got a chip on your shoulder, do you?" he grumbled with a curse. He'd been thinking about her again. All the way to town he'd been trying to exorcize her from his thoughts with little luck. Before she'd left town, she'd made him feel as if he was never going to amount to anything. It still stuck in his craw.

He kept seeing her sitting in her car while he refueled it. She hadn't even had the good grace to look at him— not to mention acknowledge that she'd once known him. Known him damned well, too.

Dawson gave that memory an angry shove away. When Annabelle Clementine had left town in a cloud of dust years ago, she'd said she was never looking back. Well, today proved that, didn't it?

Worked up over his run-in with her, he told himself he just needed a hot shower and clean clothes. But as he caught his reflection in the bathroom mirror, he came to a startled stop and had to laugh. He wouldn't even recognize himself after two weeks in a hunting camp in the Missouri Breaks.

He stared at his grizzled face and filthy, camp-worn clothes, seeing what she'd seen today. Even if she had recognized him, seeing him like that would only have confirmed what she'd thought of him all those years ago. He looked like a man who wasn't going anywhere.

Stripping down, he turned on the shower and stepped in. The warm water felt like heaven as he began to suds up in a fury. He just wanted that woman out of his hair—and his head. But his thoughts went straight as an arrow to that image of her standing beside the river. Her long blond hair gleaming in the sunlight and that black outfit hugging every unforgettable curve he'd once known so well. Growling, he turned the water to cold.

Out of the shower and toweling himself off, he looked at his reflection in the mirror again. Was it really possible that she hadn't known him? He reached for his razor, telling himself it didn't matter. With a curse, he acknowledged that he'd been lying to himself for years about his feelings for her—ever since that day he'd rescued her from his tree house when she was five.

And he'd rescued her again today, he thought with a curse. He just never learned.

ANNABELLE TOOK THE key from her pocket and opened her grandmother's front door, Mary Sue Linton at her elbow. Taking a deep breath, she stepped inside, bracing herself for more painful memories. Instead, shock stopped her cold just inside the door.

"You can't sell the house like this," Mary Sue said, stating the obvious next to her. "I thought you said your sisters cleaned everything out?"

"They said they took what they wanted." She couldn't believe what she was seeing. Her grandmother hadn't been a packrat, she'd been a hoarder. The house was crammed full of…stuff. She could barely see the floor. The rooms appeared to be filled with furniture, knick-knacks, stacks of newspapers and magazines, bags of clothing and clutter. The house looked more like a crowded old antique shop than a home. Unfortunately it didn't take a trained eye to see that all of this wasn't even junkshop worthy.

"What am I supposed to do with all of this?" she demanded. "I can't very well have a garage sale this time of year. If there was anything in all this mess worth selling." It was late November. Christmas was only weeks away.

Mary Sue shrugged. "You could hire someone to help you pack it all up. Unfortunately, the local charity shop can't take most of this. If there are things you want to save—"

"No."

"I was going to say that you could put them into a storage shed."

Annabelle was shaking her head, overwhelmed as they worked their way along the paths through the house.

"Otherwise, I could give you some names of people who might be able to help you at least haul it out to the dump."

"Great. How long is that going to take? I need to get this house on the market right away." She followed the narrow trails, going from room to room, Mary Sue on her heels, until she reached what had once been a bedroom but now looked more like a storage room where a bomb had gone off.

"This is no normal hoarding," Mary Sue said. "It looks like someone ransacked this room."

Annabelle agreed it did appear that someone had torn into all the boxes and dumped the contents on the floor. Her grandmother before she died? Her sisters when they'd come back for the funeral?

"Look at the window," Mary Sue said in a hoarse whisper as she grabbed Annabelle's arm, her fingernails digging into tender flesh.

"Ouch." She jerked free and kicked aside some of the mess to move to the window, which was now half open, the screen torn. "The lock is broken."

Behind her, Mary Sue let out a shudder. "Someone broke in."

That was the way it appeared, although she couldn't imagine in her wildest dreams why they would want to. She closed the window and turned to find Mary Sue hugging herself.

"Whoever broke in isn't here anymore," she tried to assure the Realtor. "Let's look upstairs. Maybe it's better." Unfortunately, the upstairs wasn't any better; both bedrooms were stacked full of clutter, including her grandmother's old room.

Back downstairs, she took another look at the front downstairs bedroom. It wasn't quite as full as the others. She checked the closet, found what must be her grandmother's clothing and assumed that, as Frannie got older, she'd moved downstairs.

"Could this be anymore outdated?" Mary Sue called from the kitchen.

"I think I can clean out one of the downstairs bedrooms so at least I'll have a place I can stay," Annabelle said as she joined her in the kitchen. The front bedroom downstairs had been hers growing up.

Mary Sue didn't seem to hear her. Instead, she was frowning at the clipboard she had in her hands.

*"What?"* Annabelle demanded. "Don't tell me there is another problem."

"No, not exactly. But it is strange. This is a layout of the house I got from the records department at the courthouse," she said, indicating the sheet on her clipboard. "That wall shouldn't be there."

*"What?"*

"This shows an alcove."

"An alcove? Maybe it's back there behind all the junk and you just can't see it."

Mary Sue's frown deepened. "Do you remember an alcove from when you were growing up here?"

She was supposed to remember an alcove? Seriously? "No. The plans for the house must be outdated."

"Not according to the courthouse. Your grandmother bought this house when she was in her twenties so she had it for…"

"She was seventy-six when she died, so she had it for more than fifty years." Annabelle hadn't realized how long Frannie had lived in Whitehorse until she'd seen it in the obituary that one of her sisters had sent her. It hadn't been out of kindness that Chloe had mailed it to her. Her older sister had never been that subtle. Both Chloe and Tessa Jane—TJ—had tried to make her feel guilty about their grandmother leaving her the house— let alone Annabelle missing the funeral.

"Frannie owned this house almost from the time it was built," Mary Sue was saying. "So if anyone made the changes, it had to have been your grandmother.

Why would she wall up an alcove? I wonder what's behind it?"

"Okay, you're giving me the creeps now," Annabelle said. "Clearly, you have the plans for the wrong house. Aren't there a bunch of houses along this street with similar floor plans?"

Mary Sue nodded, but didn't look convinced. "I can check at the courthouse again I guess. But you have to admit, if the plans are right, then it is more than a little odd to wall up the alcove, let alone—"

"You're letting your imagination run away with you. You *knew* my grandmother."

With a lift of one eyebrow, Mary Sue said, "She said her husband died before she moved to Whitehorse, but what if—"

"Seriously? You think my grandfather's body is stuffed in there?"

"Ever seen the play *Arsenic and Old Lace*?"

"Frannie Clementine was one of the most kind and generous people in town. She wouldn't hurt a fly." Standing just over five feet, Frannie had been a tiny, sweet-tempered woman who loved kids, garage sales and cooking. She attended church every Sunday, come rain or shine or snow.

Annabelle could tell that Mary Sue was enjoying trying to scare her. Was it any wonder that they hadn't been friends in high school?

"Just sayin'," the Realtor said, clearly trying to hide a grin. "Did you know that since her death right before Halloween last month, kids are saying that this house is haunted?"

"That's ridiculous. Just because she died in this house..." Annabelle tried to hide the shudder that moved through her at the thought. If one of her neighbors, old Inez Gilbert, hadn't come over to check on Frannie, she would have been lost in all this mess for weeks. That thought did nothing to improve the situation.

"On Halloween some kids saw what they said was a ghost moving around in the house. They said it looked like an old woman dressed in all white and—"

"Stop," Annabelle snapped, having had enough. The house was creepy as it was with all the memories, not to mention being filled to overflowing with collected junk. She really didn't need this. "It was probably Inez from next door. The woman is a horrible busybody and always has been."

If Mary Sue thought she could scare her, then she didn't know what scary was. Unfortunately, Annabelle did. It was losing a dream job and a fabulous lifestyle, and being forced to do things she'd told herself she would never do, like return to this town and all the memories that came with it.

"The house isn't haunted. There never was an alcove—"

Mary Sue tapped her clipboard. "But the plans—"

"The alcove isn't here now so that's all I care about. I need to get packing and you need to get this house sold. Just get me the names of people who will help clean it out."

Right now, though, she needed a breath of fresh air and Whitehorse had plenty of that. She stepped out onto

the front porch, letting the door close behind her. She'd
known this wouldn't be easy, but it was turning out to
be more difficult than she could have imagined. The
memories, the stories, the stupid missing alcove, not to
mention all that junk. She definitely had more pressing
things to worry about than a bunch of local kids thinking the house was haunted.

The clock was ticking, she thought, looking at her
car, the last vestige of her former life other than the
clothes on her back. She had to get this house sold.

MARY SUE GRITTED her teeth. Annabelle annoyed her
to no end. "Hasn't changed a bit," she muttered. "Get
me this, do this for me." She looked around the house,
her gaze going to the kitchen and the missing alcove. "I
hope there is a body walled up in there—and a vindic-
tive ghost who hates blondes." That would serve Annabelle right.

She felt guilty, but only a little, for trying to scare her
former classmate. But she was still puzzling over the
missing alcove as she stepped out onto the porch. Her
mother had been a Realtor. Maybe she'd ask her if she
knew anything about the old Clementine house, as it
was known around town. It sat along with a half dozen
others on a street locally and affectionately known as
Millionaire's Row. The houses were large, a lot of them
the same basic floor plan.

Mary Sue moved to the end of the porch to look back
at the rock wall that marked the property line. On the
other side of the wall was the Milk River. Between the
house and the river, though, were large trees and an ex-

panse of grass broken only by some cracked sidewalk that ended at an old garage that had seen better days.

"That should come down," she said of the dilapidated structure and marked it on her sheet on her clipboard. Through the trees, she could make out only a portion of the neighboring house's eaves in the distance. These really were beautiful old houses along this street, so private because of the old-growth trees and the huge lots. Not exactly Millionaire's Row now, but definitely prime real estate in this town.

"So where can I reach you?" Mary Sue asked, turning to Annabelle who appeared distracted. Not that she could blame her. The supermodel had quite a job before her.

"You have my cell number and you know where to find me. I'll be staying here."

*"In the house?"* Mary Sue couldn't help her surprise.

Annabelle turned to look at her. "Why *wouldn't* I stay here?"

"No reason, except…" She remembered all the clutter and the fact that Frannie had died here. Not that unusual for a woman her age, but still, add to that the walled-up alcove… Mary Sue shivered.

While she had been trying to scare Annabelle earlier, she had to admit that the house had an odd feel to it. Maybe it was just her, but there was something… Or maybe she had managed to scare herself more than she had Annabelle and all because of that discrepancy in the floor plan—and the fact that someone had broken into the house and might come back.

She mentioned this to Annabelle who only waved

away the idea. "It was probably kids. You know how teenagers are, an empty house, ghost story dares…"

Mary Sue didn't know, but she had a feeling that Annabelle was all too aware of how kids like *that* acted because she'd been one. "I just thought you'd want to stay at the hotel, since that's where your sisters stayed when they came home for the funeral."

Annabelle made an angry sound under her breath. "*They didn't stay here?* No wonder they didn't take much—let alone tell me how full this house was. I thought they were here going through things. From what I can see, they didn't take anything. You were the one who let them into the house with the key I sent you, right?"

Mary Sue sighed, wondering if Annabelle was going to blame her. "Yes, but I didn't come inside. The house was left to you. I was the one who was responsible for opening the door and making sure it was locked when they left. That was all. I wouldn't have felt comfortable going in the house without you."

"So did they take *anything*?"

"Not as far as I could tell." She shrugged. "I let them in, they went into the house, but only for a short period of time, they sat on the porch steps for a little while and then they left and I locked up. From what I saw, they took a few framed photographs, but I think that was about all."

Annabelle looked as if she was going to blow a gasket. "I should have known they wouldn't be of any help. That's just great. Well, they're not getting anything now. Not that there is anything worth keeping in there. From what I've seen, most of the stuff is on the way to the dump just as soon as I can get it loaded up. I'll need help right away. Did you make those calls yet?"

Mary Sue tried not to bristle. "You do realize that tomorrow is Thanksgiving, right?" she asked. "And the day after that is Black Friday, when a lot of people in town will be shopping, either locally or driving the three hours to Billings." Billings was the largest city in Montana and two hundred miles to the south. Mary Sue was planning to go down to shop with a couple of friends, spending the night at a hotel and making a trip out of it.

"Your point?"

"It's going to be hard to find anyone to help this time of year," she said, and added quickly before Annabelle could argue. "But let me make a few quick calls." She hurriedly stepped off the porch and walked down the cracked driveway toward her car, phone in hand. Even though it was now close to freezing outside, she didn't want to go back into the house. Nor did she want Annabelle to hear her phone conversations. When she told people who they would be working for, she expected them to balk.

A few minutes later, she returned to the porch where Annabelle was pacing. The model looked cold, but no wonder, since she was inappropriately dressed for Montana weather. Mary Sue guessed that she wasn't anxious to go back inside the house, either. "I found a couple of men who are willing to help for thirty dollars an hour."

"*Thirty dollars an hour?* I'm not asking them to re-model the house." Annabelle looked through the window with a shake of the head as if calculating how many hours work was in there. "Forget it," she said with a sigh. "I'll do the packing myself. Where can I find some boxes?"

"Behind the town recycling center. But you aren't going to be able to get very many into that car of yours. Are you sure you don't want—"

"I'll figure it out."

"Okay, but once you get everything boxed up, you're going to need a truck to take it either to the dump or a storage unit, if you decide to keep some of it."

"Got it. I'll deal with all that once it's boxed up."

"I have plans, otherwise…" Otherwise what? Did she really feel guilty about not offering to help? If Annabelle was too cheap to hire help, that was her problem.

With a wave of her hand, her former classmate dismissed her.

"All right, then let me know when the house is ready to go on the market," Mary Sue said, not about to mention that the place would need to be cleaned. A nice coat of fresh paint in the rooms would also help. But she didn't feel that Annabelle was up to hearing more bad news right now and Mary Sue wasn't up to giving it.

Anyway, she was anxious to talk to her mother. As she walked to her car, her clipboard in hand, she tried to convince herself that she'd gotten the wrong floor plan from the courthouse.

Except she knew better. She prided herself on being thorough. Frannie had walled up the alcove. But why? And what was in the closed-up space?

"SHOULDN'T YOU BE ASLEEP?" the assisted-living nurse asked from his doorway.

Bernard "Bernie the Hawk" McDougal gave her the smile that had worked on women since he was a boy. Even at eighty-nine, the old mobster still could make a woman blush with no more than a wink and a grin. There might be snow on the roof, but it was still plenty hot down in the furnace.

"Just finishing up here," he told her from his desk and waited until she moved on before he picked up the scissors again.

He pulled the newspaper clipping toward him, still shocked that he'd discovered it online while surfing for obits of women of a certain age. The moment he'd seen this one, he'd printed it out, but the resolution wasn't good so he'd called the newspaper where it had run— the *Milk River Courier*—and had the paper overnighted to him.

It had arrived this afternoon while he was napping. When he'd awakened, he'd seen the envelope waiting for him on his desk and quickly torn into it. Inside he'd found the complete edition of that week's Whitehorse, Montana, newspaper—all four pages of it.

Now he studied the face in the obituary mug shot. The photo didn't do her justice. The one he'd seen on the internet had been much more flattering.

But no photo of his Baby Doll could hold a candle to the woman in the flesh—especially back when she was young. She'd been a blonde beauty. Tiny and gorgeous, she'd been exquisite. The kind of woman who stopped traffic and turned heads. She'd certainly turned his, he thought with a curse. And the things she'd put him through from the first time he'd laid eyes on her.

That was something else about her that had attracted her to him. She wasn't intimidated by him or any of his goons. Oh, that woman had a mouth on her. She could cut a man down to size as if her tongue was a switchblade.

He chuckled to himself. He'd wanted her and would have married her, but she wasn't having any of that. She liked being mysterious. Hell, he'd never known her real name. That first night at the party, he'd seen right away that she and her friend had crashed his little get-together on the posh rooftop of his favorite New York City restaurant. He'd thought about booting the two of them, but there was something about her.

She'd flirted with him but refused to tell him who she was, as if she thought he'd call her daddy to have her picked up and taken home. A few minutes with her and that was the last thing he planned to do.

"Okay, you want to play it coy? You'll just be my Baby Doll, then," he'd said, knowing even then that he had to have her.

"Baby Doll? I like that," she'd said, coming off older than she was. She hadn't been more than seventeen. Jailbait. Like that had stopped him. He had a reputation for going after whatever he wanted—and getting it. But then, so did Baby Doll as it turned out.

Opening the scissors, he began to slice the paper around her mug shot. Bernie couldn't stand sloppiness.

He liked things done a certain way. It had saved his life more than once and kept him from being behind bars.

Now he found himself looking into her eyes, remembering. This was her. There was no doubt about it. He'd thought he found her before, but this time… He wished he had been able to find a photograph of her when she was younger but there was nothing on the internet. Francesca Marie Clementine had kept a low profile. Another reason he was convinced that this woman was his Baby Doll.

Oh, those blue eyes. The memories of her in his arms. Just being with her had felt like living on the edge, she'd been that kind of woman. She kept his blood revved up. He'd known he could never get enough of her. He'd asked her to marry him more times than he liked to remember. He shook his head. While he'd only known her a short while, he'd thought he could trust her with his life, his secrets—and his loot. His first mistake.

That was the problem, wasn't it? he thought as he clipped the photo free from the newspaper. He'd trusted a woman who hadn't even trusted him enough to tell him her real name.

"Come on, Baby Doll, tell me your name," he used to tease her. "We can't get married until I know exactly who you are."

"Oh, you know who I am." She'd smiled that coy smile of hers and said, "I'm Bernie McDougal's Baby Doll. That's enough. For now." Her look had been a promise of a lot more to come and he'd been a goner. Oh, the swanky parties they'd attended, the fur coats and fancy dresses he'd clothed her in, the expensive champagne they'd guzzled, the money they'd burned through. Nothing was too good for his Baby Doll.

His stomach roiled at the memory. She'd blindsided him from the beginning, he thought, able to admit it now, more than fifty years later. He'd thought she was young and naïve. He'd never seen it coming.

The obit was short, but it did provide some useful information, such as where she'd been all these years—and that she was survived by her three granddaughters, Annabelle Clementine, Tessa Jane Clementine (TJ St. Clair) and Chloe Clementine. No husband. That didn't surprise him.

He'd had to look up the town on the internet. White-horse, Montana. It surprised him that she'd disappeared to some wide spot out West. He'd always thought of her living it up in Paris or London, or even New York City where it had all begun. It was why he'd looked for her in the faces of every woman he'd passed all these years.

But Baby Doll had always been full of surprises, hadn't she? He still couldn't believe that she'd evaded him. He'd had his men looking for her as well as his associates. He'd put a price on her pretty head. And still nothing. It was as if she'd stepped off the face of the earth.

But he'd finally found her. The problem was, it seemed too late. She was dead. Which meant that she'd probably taken their secret to the grave. It filled him with regret. He would have loved to look into her eyes one last time before he killed her.

He took her photo, stuck a pin between her eyes and put it up on the bulletin board next to his desk. As he started to throw the rest of the newspaper away, his gaze lit on the name *Clementine* again.

It appeared to be a real estate ad. Moving the paper where he could see the ad, he saw that it read *Clementine Place*. His breath came out on a laugh. Of course. She'd owned a house and now it was for sale. A house where she'd kept her secrets. He told himself not to get his hopes up, and yet he was reaching for his phone since it was still early out in Montana.

Francesca's house was for sale? Why hadn't he thought of that? There were some things she wouldn't have been able to take with her. That is, if she'd still had them when she'd died. She could have gone through everything a long time ago. Probably had. But there was only one way to find out.

He dialed the number of the Realtor who was selling the house. The newspaper was a week old. The house could have sold by now.

A woman named Mary Sue Linton answered on the third ring.

"I'm calling about a house you have for sale," he said. "I believe it's called Clementine Place?"

"That's right. It just went on the market. What can I tell you about it?"

He had the photo of the house in front of him. But he couldn't imagine Baby Doll living somewhere like that. It was too common after the penthouse they'd shared. It all came down to that one question that had niggled at him all these years. Why? Why take off like she had—let alone end up where she had? Which led to his second big question. What had she done with what she'd stolen from him?

"I'd like to send someone to look at it in the next few days," he said. "Is that possible?"

"It's not quite ready to show."

Really? "I don't care what kind of shape it's in."

"One of the relatives is in the process of cleaning everything out. I'm afraid Frannie was a…collector." Yes, she'd collected a few things from him before she'd left. "But the house will be pristine in a few weeks if you'd like to see it then."

Frannie? "You say a relative is cleaning it out?"

"Her granddaughter, Annabelle."

His old heart thumped hard against his ribs. What if she'd already thrown it out? She had to be stopped. "Then I'll check back with you."

"That would be ideal."

He hung up and made a call. "I need to see you. *Now.*"

Oh, Baby Doll, he said to himself as he disconnected. The woman had thought she'd outfoxed him. Soon she would be turning over in her grave. As for her granddaughter, she could be joining Frannie very soon.

# Chapter Three

Dawson hadn't driven by the old Clementine place in years. After he'd cleaned up, he'd driven into town since there was still some daylight left in the winter day and his brother had called wanting to hear about his hunting trip. He'd told himself he wasn't going near Annabelle's grandmother's house, but it was as if his pickup had a mind of its own.

There was a time that this neighborhood had been his second home. That was back when his best friend lived two doors down from Frannie Clementine's house. Back when he and his best friend had built a tree house only to find five-year-old Annabelle in it and unable to get down.

With a bark of a laugh, he reminded himself that she hadn't been filled with gratitude that time he'd saved her, either.

He slowed his pickup, surprised how long it had been since he'd driven through this neighborhood. His best friend had moved away years ago and once Annabelle left…

The house, on so-called Millionaire's Row on the

west side of town, sat on a huge lot surrounded by massive trees. Behind it, the water of the Milk River curved slowly past. An old single-car garage stood off to the side, looking like it needed to be torn down.

He pulled up on the opposite side of the street. There was a For Sale sign in the yard, which shouldn't have come as a surprise. Mystery solved. Of course that was what had brought Annabelle back. She was planning to get rid of the house—the only thing still tethering her to Whitehorse now that her grandmother was gone.

Pulling under the protective boughs of a huge evergreen, he left the engine running and took in the home. He was wondering what Annabelle could get for the place when he saw a woman in a bandanna, a gaudy sweatshirt and a pair of baggy jeans come out. She carried a large box out the front door to the side of the porch closest to the driveway. Even from a distance, he could tell that the woman was covered in dust and dirt. So Annabelle had hired help. That, too, shouldn't have surprised him, although he didn't recognize the woman.

As she set the box at the open end of the porch, she stood to stretch, as if her back bothered her. A lock of blond hair escaped from beneath the bandanna. With a shock, he realized what he was seeing. *Annabelle?*

The sight of the supermodel looking like a janitor made him laugh and shake his head in disbelief. He was tempted to take a photo with his cell phone. But he could just imagine how horrified she would be if he did. He had barely recognized her, and not just because he suspected Annabelle had never done a day's manual labor in her life. Surely she wasn't packing up the entire house by herself.

But as he looked around, he saw that the only vehicle near the place was the silver sports car. Nor did anyone else emerge from the house carrying boxes as he sat watching, truck engine running. Why hadn't she hired help? It was so unlike her.

A thought struck him like a swift kick to the shin. She'd said she'd forgotten to get gas, but what if... The idea was so preposterous that he laughed out loud as he put his pickup into gear to drive away. Whatever Annabelle was up to, it had nothin' to do with him. He didn't even know why he'd driven by.

His cell phone rang, making him jump. He really wasn't good at this cloak-and-dagger stuff. He hit the brakes and quickly answered as he watched Annabelle put down another box, stretch and go back inside. As she glanced in his direction, he slowly let out the clutch and eased the pickup down the street, making sure he kept his head turned. The last thing he wanted was for her to think that he had any interest in her.

"You on your way?" his brother asked without preamble.

He'd lost track of time. "I am. Be right there." He disconnected, hoping his brother's invitation was only about having a beer. The way news traveled around this county, by now everyone could know that Annabelle Clementine was back in town—his brother Luke included. And that was a subject he didn't want to discuss.

Luke was already sitting on a bar stool at the Mint when he walked in. Seeing him coming, Luke ordered him a Moose Drool and patted the stool next to him. "Some pretty nice weather for November, huh?"

"Uh-huh," Dawson said, groaning inside. Luke was grinning like a jackass and it had nothing to do with the weather.

"Annabelle Clementine is back in town," his brother blurted, as if unable to hold it in a second longer.

"Who?" Dawson asked innocently and took a sip of the beer the bartender set in front of him. Luke was as subtle as a horseshoe to the head. At least he'd been smart enough to know that Dawson would need a beer.

*"Who?"* Luke echoed. "Annabelle Clementine, or as you used to call her…Annie. You aren't going to tell me that you've forgotten about the woman who—" His brother stopped and gave him a you-had-me-there-for-a-minute grin. "So, you already heard?" He sounded disappointed.

"Actually, I saw her."

*"No kiddin'?* She still gorgeous? She say why she's back?"

Dawson ran his thumb around the top of his beer bottle for a moment. Something stopped him from telling his brother about siphoning gas out of his pickup to practically fill her fancy sports car. "Saw her packing up at her grandmother's house. She's got the place for sale." He took a sip of his beer.

"You just happened to be in that neighborhood, did you?" Luke couldn't seem to get that goofy grin off his face. "She say how long she's staying?"

"I said I *saw* her. Didn't say I made a point of talking to her. So I wouldn't know, but I think it's a pretty good assumption that she'll be hightailing it out of town just as quickly as she can," he said without looking at his brother.

"Why didn't you talk to her?" Luke asked.

"Why would I?"

"After all these years, I would think you'd be curious. Maybe it isn't just her grandmother's house that brought her back. Maybe—"

"It's just her grandmother's house."

"You can't know that. Maybe—"

"So, what's the plan for tomorrow?" Dawson asked, hoping to change the subject. Thinking about Annabelle gave him a headache. Talking about her was even worse. It had been years since he'd called her Annie, let alone allowed himself to even say the word. Annie was the woman he fell in love with. Annabelle was...well, she was a supermodel he didn't know, didn't want to know.

"Tomorrow?" Luke asked, as if confused by the quick change of subject.

*"Thanksgiving Day."*

"Don't remind me." Luke took a drink of his beer, clearly upset that this was all he was going to get. He sighed. "I haven't gotten my deer yet. But you know Mom. Said not to be late. She's invited some of the neighbors."

Dawson nodded, smiling to himself at the thought of their mother. There was no one quite like Wilhelmina "Willie" Rogers. She'd managed to raise both of her sons on her own after their father died when they were boys—and run the ranch, as well. When it came to anyone who needed a hot meal, Willie was always ready to rustle something up. His mother equated love with food. She spent half her time making casseroles for anyone who'd fallen on hard times or families who'd had an illness. Anyone in town die? The family would have a dish on their doorstep within the hour.

"Mom said we both better be there," Luke said. "She already read me the riot act about going deer hunting beforehand. Speaking of hunting, how'd you do down in the Breaks? Get anything worth bringing home and stringin' up?"

Dawson shook his head. "I saw one big buck, but didn't get a shot." The truth was, he loved hiking around looking for deer and elk, but when he still had plenty of meat in the freezer, he wasn't much for killing anything. He wasn't a trophy hunter.

Two weeks in hunting camp with some buddies, though, was a tradition he wasn't apt to miss. He liked sleeping out under the stars, working his way through rugged country during the day, eating food cooked over a camp stove and sitting around the fire later, listening to his friends' outrageous stories before climbing into his bedroll. He always slept like the dead at hunting camp.

Not that he wasn't glad to get home to a hot shower and his own bed.

"Any idea how much the old Clementine place might go for?" Luke asked.

"Haven't given it any thought."

"Still, you have to admit it's strange that Annabelle wouldn't let Mary Sue handle it so she didn't have to come back here," Luke said. His brother was dating Mary Sue's younger sister, Sally. "Unless the house wasn't the only reason she's back," he said, clearly baiting him. "Kinda makes you wonder, doesn't it?"

"What makes me wonder is what *your* interest in all this is," Dawson said and looked over at his brother.

"Actually, I find your apparent so-called *lack* of interest more fascinating. You don't think I didn't know how you felt about her? Now she's back. You aren't even going to stop by her place and talk to her?" Luke shook his head. "My big brother, as it turns out, is a coward."

"It's not going to work," Dawson said and drained the rest of his beer.

"The brother I knew would have given his left arm for that woman," Luke said. "He wouldn't pass up a possible second chance to be with her. You telling me you don't still feel somethin'?"

Dawson shook his head as he stood. "I'm not tellin' you anything. I'll let my walkin' out of here speak for itself. Thanks for the beer."

Luke sighed. "Fine, have it your way, you stubborn jackass. But you're going to be sorry."

"I've been sorry before. Tell Mom I'll stop by early tomorrow to see if she needs any help."

"You always have to be the good son, don't you? I'm going deer huntin'. Save me a place at the table just in case I get something and run late." The door closed on his last words.

Even as Dawson started his pickup, he knew he was going to do it. And it made him madder than hell. He turned down the street. It wasn't late, but it was already dark this time of year. Deep shadows hunkered in the trees. The temperature had dropped.

As he drove by her house, he saw that the light was on. There were more boxes stacked up under the porch roof. He turned out his headlights as he stopped across the street again. Several large pines blocked most of the house, but he would get glimpses of her inside working.

There was still no sign of anyone helping her. "What's going on, Annie?" he asked in the dark cab of his truck. If she didn't get out of town before the next snowstorm, she probably wouldn't be able to in that impractical car of hers. He doubted she had snow tires on it since she'd been living in California. Not that they would help much. A car like that would get high-centered on the first snowdrift across the highway. Hell, she'd be lucky if she could get out of her driveway.

Dawson reminded himself that it wasn't his problem. And yet he couldn't help thinking about what his brother had said back at the bar. Unfortunately, he'd already been a fool when it came to her. He liked to think he was too smart to do it again as he watched her pass in front of the large picture window. She looked exhausted. How many hours had she been packing up her grandmother's things by herself?

But even from this distance, he could see the determination in her expression, in the way she moved. There had never been a more stubborn woman, he thought, as he turned on his headlights again and headed for the ranch.

ANNABELLE HURT ALL OVER. She closed another box on more of her grandmother's chipped and cracked knick-knacks, but realized she was too tired to take it out to

.J. Daniels49

the porch. For hours, she'd been boxing up her grandmother's junk. Now she looked around the room with growing discouragement. She'd thought she was making progress, but she hadn't even made a dent in all this...stuff.

Earlier she'd removed what she could from the front bedroom. Her grandmother had been using the one in the back of the house opposite the shared bathroom. Apparently, she'd turned the bedroom Annabelle had chosen into an extra wardrobe. An array of ugly, gaudy sweatshirts was hanging in the closet. Each was bedazzled with anything shiny you could tack onto it. Where did the woman find these horrific things? A lot of them were seasonal, with Santas, elves, Christmas lights, overdecorated wreaths, even an Easter egg one that was so bright it could put an eye out.

Not wanting to ruin the last of the good clothes that she hadn't sold to pay for the trip north, she'd changed into one of the less garish ones, a sweatshirt with a bejeweled clown face, along with a pair of her grandmother's pull-on jeans that she had to tie around her waist so they'd stay up, a pair of sneakers and socks with lacy tops. They'd do to work in.

After she'd decluttered the bedroom, she cleaned. She'd discovered some laundered sheets and made the bed so it would be ready for tonight. Then she'd gone down to the recycling building in town and loaded as many boxes as she could into her car by putting smaller ones into larger ones and holding some out the window as she drove.

Back at the house, she'd started dumping the worst of the junk into boxes and carrying them out to the porch.

Now she just wanted to sit down. *You were so right, Mary Sue. I really could have used some help.* But not at thirty dollars an hour. And no one was going to work for her with only the promise of getting paid *after* the house sold.

She wandered into the kitchen, one of the only rooms that had chairs that weren't covered with junk. As full as the place was, she couldn't help but be thankful to her grandmother. Frannie had never had a lot of money, but in the will she'd made sure that the taxes and utilities were paid six months in advance.

Clearly, she'd known what a job it was going to be to clean out this house and sell it.

Brushing an errant lock of hair back from her dirty face, Annabelle wondered if her grandmother had also somehow figured that she was going to need financial help. Six months was generous. Frannie had to have known that Annabelle wouldn't be staying that long. But it definitely allowed her time to get the house sold.

She glanced around the kitchen, tempted to fill another box with the ceramic knickknacks that crowded the windowsill. Her grandmother had saved *everything*. Was it an old lady thing? Or had her grandmother lost her mind before the end? She couldn't understand how the woman had been able to live here with junk piled waist high throughout the house. It seemed at odds with the woman who'd raised Annabelle most of her life.

But it was also odd that her grandmother had willed the house to her and not her sisters. It still bothered her.

"Why, Grandma Frannie? Why leave the house to just me?" she asked the knickknacks. Several frogs looked back at her with big, dusty eyes. Maybe TJ was right. Frannie had left the house to the granddaughter she thought would need the most help.

At the time, Annabelle had been furious at such an insinuation. Now she wondered if her grandmother hadn't been the only one who'd expected her to fail. Maybe everyone had seen it coming but Annabelle herself.

For whatever the reason, this house was now hers and unless she got it sold and soon… She shook her head, stood and reached for the ceramic bric-a-brac.

Her stomach rumbled. She hadn't even thought about food—until this moment. For years she'd had to watch her weight. She still wasn't used to being able to eat anything she wanted. Now she could give in to her hunger. It was a new feeling. One that signaled more than anything that she would never be modeling again. Too bad she couldn't afford to eat.

She pushed that thought away. Looking down at the hideous clothes she was wearing, she told herself that she couldn't go to the grocery store, even in Whitehorse, in this outfit—even if she had any cash. She stood for a moment, feeling lost and close to tears. As she put one of the ceramic creatures into the box she was loading, she spied a container that her grandmother had used for her grocery money.

She was reminded of the time Grandma Frannie had caught her red-handed with her fingers in it and felt a stab of remorse for even having thought about taking the money, let alone getting caught. But mostly what she felt was regret that she hadn't come back to see the grandmother who'd loved her so much.

That day, her hand literally in the cookie jar, Annabelle had fished around for an excuse. Her grandmother had stopped her and said, "If you're going to steal, then own it. Same with getting caught," her grandmother had said. "Lying and sniveling makes you look weak."

With a sigh, she now lifted the lid of the container, telling herself it would be empty. Reaching inside, her fingers brushed something. She pulled out a handful of crinkled-up twenties and began to cry.

"Grandma," she said, her voice breaking. She swallowed the lump in her throat and wiped at her tears. Frannie had known she was going to need money. She *was* the one her grandmother had known would fail. As much as that hurt, her heart filled to bursting with love for her grandmother, who was still looking out for her after all these years. Because someone needed to, that was for sure.

There were enough bills to keep her from going hungry for a while. She said a whispered thank-you to her grandmother and glanced at her watch. Did she really have the energy to shower and change to go to the grocery store to get something to eat?

The answer was a resounding no. If she sneaked in and out of the only grocery store in town quickly, hopefully she wouldn't see anyone she knew.

ROBERT "ROB" MCDOUGAL saw that it was his uncle calling and ignored the call. The old mobster probably just wanted to bitch about the way-too-expensive assisted-living facility where he'd been the past four years.

Since Rob was paying almost twenty grand a month to keep him in the resort-like place, he didn't have much sympathy. It was a deal his old man had made with the "family."

Rob wasn't stupid enough to renege on the agreement, since that would get him killed. But he didn't have to listen to the old man's constant complaining. Nor was he in the mood to indulge his uncle.

But when his phone rang once again and he saw that it was Bernie calling yet another time, he finally listened to the original message his uncle had left.

"I have a job for you. A real one. Get your butt out here. This is urgent family business."

Urgent family business? Rob groaned. What now? He didn't bother to call his uncle back. He simply texted that he was on his way to Golden Years Retirement Living and Spa.

The moment he walked into his uncle's room, the old codger patted the arm of his wheelchair and said, "Let's take a walk."

In his uncle's generation that might have meant he was about to die. But he didn't think Bernie had a gun on him or a garrote or even a butter knife from the kitchen. But you never knew.

"What's this about?" Rob asked impatiently as he pushed the old man's wheelchair out to the canal after getting a special pass at the main desk to do so. It was hot as hell, even though it was late at night, but it often was this far south. Florida. He hated it. He missed the change of seasons up north. But as long as Bernie was alive… And the old codger didn't seem to be aging in the least.

"Isn't this far enough?" Rob asked, swatting at a mosquito as he kept an eye out for alligators. Each year down here alligators attacked ten people on average. They snatched pets from the sides of pools, grabbed little kids and even ate a few adults, twenty-three since 1948, he'd read. Walking along the canal always made him nervous.

His uncle finally signaled they could stop. Looking around he checked to make sure they were alone. They were. Rob was losing patience. His shirt was soaked with sweat and sticking to his back. He swatted at another bug flying around his head and swore under his breath.

"The Marco Polo Heist," Bernie said.

Rob felt his stomach twist. He'd grown up without a father because of that heist. Everything had gone perfectly until an off-duty guard had shown up. His father and one of the other thieves had been killed. Only one of the thieves had gotten away clean—Bernie. The cops had known Bernie was involved but they'd never been able to prove it.

Bernie had walked away with the loot—which was never recovered since, according to his uncle, it had been stolen right out from under his nose. It had been the only black stain on the mobster's otherwise glowing criminal career—and something that remained stuck in the old man's craw.

"I have a lead on the goods," his uncle said.

After more than fifty years and a lot of blind alleys and wild-goose chases? Rob stared at him. "It just came to you?"

Bernie cuffed him in the back. "Don't be a damned fool. I know you think I'm getting senile, but I'm as sharp as a shank."

Right, Rob thought as he watched the old man dig a newspaper clipping out of his pocket.

"That's her," his uncle said, handing him the black-and-white photo. "Francesca Clementine." When Rob had no reaction, he added impatiently, "Baby Doll."

The notorious Baby Doll. Rob wanted to laugh. He'd had to hear about her all of his adult life. The moll who'd broken Bernie's heart and stolen a king's fortune from him.

"That's her?" He couldn't help being skeptical. They'd been here before.

His uncle nodded and handed him the obit. He read it, trying not to roll his eyes. "Whitehorse, Montana?" He couldn't be serious.

Bernie smiled. "Her house is coming up for sale."

"You want me to buy the house?"

"Hell, no. Too obvious. We don't want to call attention to any of this. The Feds are still watching me." Rob doubted this but said nothing. "There are too many people still looking for the loot, you know what I'm saying?"

Just like they were still looking for Jimmy Hoffa.

"You need to leave right away," Bernie said, keeping his voice down, apparently afraid the Feds were listening from the mangroves beyond the canal. They'd had to come all the way out here by the canal with the wild alligators because his uncle was convinced that his room was bugged. "I think you can handle this alone. Better that way."

Rob nodded, telling himself he wasn't going to Montana on some wild-goose chase.

"I'm depending on you," Bernie said and grabbed his hand to squeeze it hard. "I trust you, Robby."

"Rob," he corrected for the millionth time. Nor had he been chosen because his uncle trusted him. There was no one else who would do it. He had been appointed his uncle's babysitter. Not that the family didn't still fear Bernie. The old man had his connections. It was why Rob came when his uncle called, eventually. But Montana?

The doctor had said Bernie didn't have more than a year to live. But that was four years ago. Tough as old pigskin and meaner than a junkyard dog, the old man had defied modern science with just stubborn determination alone, Rob thought.

"I'm honored that you would trust me to take care of this," he said.

His uncle chuckled and met his eye. "Honored. And smart. You know what will happen to you if you don't come back with my goods."

*His* goods. Arrogant bastard. "Let's say this dame is your…Baby Doll."

"Don't call her a dame, okay?"

"What if she still didn't have any of it when she died?" Rob asked for the sake of argument. "What if she's been selling it off? After all, it's been over fifty years."

Bernie shook his head. "I would have heard if any of it had turned up. She took all of it, the cash, the jewels, the gold. I'm betting she still had it when she died. Just to show me," he said, admiration in his tone. "She willed the house to one of her granddaughters, someone named Annabelle Clementine. The Realtor made it sound like I should know who she was."

Rob shrugged. "Never heard of her."

"Apparently she's getting the house ready to sell. Take care of her and soon. She might throw out something not realizing what it is. Just don't call attention to yourself or her. I shouldn't have to spell it out for you."

"No," Rob said. But he hadn't done any wet work in years. He didn't want to start again. "Tomorrow is Thanksgiving—"

His uncle shot him a look of disbelief and the rest of the words in Rob's mouth dried up. "When you find my loot you'll want to take off with the whole lot, but you won't. You know why?"

He shook his head even though they'd had this discussion before, since his uncle never got tired of telling him.

"Because there's a curse on the loot, but nothing like the curse that would be on you. Take me back to my room and then get on a plane. You can't waste any time. If that house sells before you get there…or the granddaughter finds the goods…"

Rob nodded since there was nothing else he could do.

"There's one more thing," Bernie said. "I doubt I'm

the only one to recognize Baby Doll. Nor am I the only one who's been looking all these years." Rob doubted that was the case but kept his trap shut. "Which means you won't be alone even if the Feds aren't wise to her. There's the insurance company guy who had to pay out all those years ago, not to mention the museum curator who swore he'd get his priceless jewels back and see me in prison."

Rob didn't bother to mention that both of those guys were probably dead by now.

"So watch your back," his uncle said. "If they recognized Baby Doll like I did… You know our photos were all over the society pages. Me and Baby Doll at the swankiest parties. She was some woman."

DAWSON KICKED AROUND his house, unable to settle more than a few minutes in any one place. He'd cleaned the kitchen after making himself some dinner, washed his hunting clothing, unpacked all his gear and even put clean sheets on his bed.

He'd been looking forward to that bed all the way from the hunting camp, but even though he was bone-weary tired, he knew he wouldn't be able to sleep. Sadie didn't have that problem. She was curled up on her bed in front of the fireplace, snoring softly.

At a hard knock on his door, he started. His first thought was Annabelle. She'd come to thank him for the gas and apologize for not saying something earlier. His heart began to pound until he reminded himself how unlikely that was. He told himself it better not be Luke with more news about Annabelle. He thought about not answering the door, but the knock was so insistent…

He opened the door and blinked when he saw that it was his neighbor from the adjoining county. "Cull?"

"Sorry to bother you so late," the cowboy and horse rancher said. "I was riding fence earlier and you've got some barbed wire down that I thought I better warn you about. I did what I could, but I'm worried you're going to have cattle out on the county road if you can't get it fixed soon."

"Thanks for the heads-up." He liked Cull McGraw. He liked all the McGraws, actually, and was glad to have them as neighbors. Anyone else might not have bothered to tell him until his cattle were running wild. "You want to come in? I think there's a couple of beers in the fridge." Suddenly he didn't want to be alone.

"Thanks, but I need to get on home," Cull said, and he realized his neighbor was probably anxious to get home to his wife. "Maybe some other time."

He closed the door and turned back to his empty house. Empty. Funny, but he'd never thought of it that way until… He swore. Until Annabelle's return. Cursing himself, he began to turn out lights. After making sure the screen was on the fireplace, he headed for bed.

Behind him, he heard the soft patter of four feet as Sadie decided to join him. He told himself the pup was all he needed for company as he heard her lie down on the floor at the foot of his bed.

But the moment he was between the cool sheets,

his thoughts spun back to Annabelle, his first love, his first lover. What was he going to have to do to get her out of his system?

## *Chapter Four*

Whitehorse, Montana. Rob swore as he sat for a moment in the dark in the parking lot of the expensive nursing home. Unfortunately, this wasn't the first time Bernie had been convinced he'd found Baby Doll. Before, it had been some old woman in Maine. Then one in California. Another in Maryland. Oh, and that one in Tennessee.

Now Whitehorse, Montana? He'd gone on too many wild-goose chases, all of them dead ends. None of the women had been Baby Doll. None of them had had the loot. All they had in common was that they were six feet under now.

He pulled the photocopied snapshot and obit from his pocket and looked at them again. Francesca Clementine? At least he wouldn't have to kill this one—she was already dead. But the granddaughter wasn't, he reminded himself.

He debated not going and telling the old man that he had and that Francesca Clementine wasn't his Baby Doll. It would break the old man's heart, but it wasn't the first time. After all, what were the chances that this

Francesca Clementine had even been to New York City, let alone had a love affair with a mobster and stolen a king's ransom in already stolen loot? Less than nil.

So why waste his time? Just give it a few days and then report back to Bernie... It was a gamble, though. He suspected the old man had Alzheimer's or dementia and his brain was more pickled than his aunt's canned beets.

But that didn't mean Bernie wasn't dangerous. He still could make Rob's life a living hell. That's if he didn't just cut bait and have Rob killed.

He considered what to do. The old man was crazy. If he found out that Rob hadn't gone to Montana...

Swearing, he pulled out his cell phone and called the airport for a ticket to the closest airport—Billings, Montana, some three hours away from Whitehorse.

This, he thought, was going to be the worst wild-goose chase ever. Montana in the winter. For the grand-daughter's sake, he hoped the old man had gotten it wrong again and he could prove it quickly.

ANNABELLE'S PLAN, WHEN she left California had been to sneak back into town, if at all possible. She'd thought she could sell her grandmother's house and be gone before anyone noticed. Now, as she drove the few blocks to the grocery, she realized how foolish that had been.

Whitehorse was so small that it didn't even have a stoplight. The closest big-box store was three hours away—and that was when the roads weren't icy or under construction. To say that the small rural town was in the middle of nowhere was an understatement. Sometimes in the winter the highways out of town would close because of a blizzard and they'd be trapped until the plows could get through.

That was one of Annabelle's worries. That she would get snowed in here before she could sell her grandmother's house and she ran completely out of money. Meanwhile, she just hoped she didn't see anyone she knew. But the way she was dressed, she hardly recognized herself, she thought, as she straightened the bandanna she'd decided to leave covering her blond hair.

Parking at the side of the grocery store, she turned off the engine and sat for a moment. Only a few people came and went. It was late and the store would close soon. She saw a few older people who could have been familiar but they didn't pay her any mind. A couple of teenaged boys eyed her car, but didn't give her a second glance.

Her stomach growling, she finally climbed out, locked her car and headed inside. Whitehorse was the kind of place where everyone returned the grocery carts. No one would dream of leaving theirs outside for fear someone would see them and they'd be the talk of the town.

Once inside the store, everyone was always very polite. There was no cart bumping, no angry looks, let alone words. This was Whitehorse. People here were beyond civilized.

Fortunately, the first aisle she went down was empty of people. She considered what she needed. Some time ago, on one of those rare occasions when she'd had too much to drink and was feeling nostalgic, she'd called home. Her grandmother had told her that the biggest news in town was that the grocery store had expanded to include a deli.

But the store still seemed small, the aisles narrow, and at one corner of the store, she swore the floor dropped a good three inches toward the back wall. Now that she was here, she felt overwhelmed. She'd never cooked, even though her grandmother had encouraged her to learn.

"You might be hungry someday," Frannie had said, making Annabelle realize that her grandmother had apparently seen this all coming.

Her sister TJ loved to cook. Chloe loved to bake. Annabelle had realized early on that there was no need for her to learn either skill if someone else cooked and baked. Even at a young age, she'd believed she would never have to cook for herself—not with the life she had planned—and that had been the case. For a while.

Faced with fending for herself in the kitchen now, she didn't know where to begin. Her grandmother had gone down to the senior center for her meals. Food-wise, the cupboards were bare.

Catching a whiff of something that smelled already cooked, she followed her nose and was delighted to find the new deli. She peered through the glass, her mouth watering, even though the deli was a far cry from the grocery stores she was used to.

"I'll take some of that," she said pointing at the breaded chicken. "And some of that," she said of chopped salad. Not having to worry about calories any-more, she feared she wouldn't be able to stop once she started eating real food again. She pointed out a few more things and happily put the containers in her cart.

"I should get something for breakfast," she said to herself spying the pastries. Lemon-filled donuts. Cream-cheese-laced rolls. Maple sticks. She hadn't faced such tough decisions in years.

"Annabelle?"

The voice behind her made her freeze in mid-drool. The years seemed to disappear and she was a tongue-tied, knobby-kneed teen again.

As she turned, Wilhelmina Rogers said, "If it isn't my favorite almost daughter-in-law." Dawson's mother threw her arms around her, hugging her as if she hadn't seen her in years. She hadn't.

*Almost daughter-in-law.* "Willie." It was all she could get out. Willie's reaction to seeing her again was surprising. Shocking, actually. Annabelle had just assumed that Willie would hate her after what she did to Dawson. The woman's greeting made her feel…loved and forgiven and guilty. Tears filled her eyes as she was enveloped by the long and lean ranchwoman's strong arms.

"Let me look at you," Willie said as she held Annabelle at arm's length and gave her the once-over. "You look good enough to eat, although I'm going to have to fatten you up before I do," she said with a hearty laugh. She instantly sobered. "Seriously, it is so good to see you."

All Annabelle could do was nod and fight tears. She'd always loved Dawson's mom. Maybe if things had been different… Who was she kidding? Maybe if *she'd* been different. Maybe if she'd wanted something different. But back then, staying in Whitehorse hadn't been an option. It would have felt like settling. It would have felt as if she wasn't good enough to leave and make it. Like she would have failed without even trying. Did she really feel all that different, even now?

"I expect to see you at my house tomorrow at 11:45 a.m. on the dot," Willie ordered.

"Tomorrow?" Annabelle parroted, feeling off-balance and confused.

"Thanksgiving! Don't even bother arguing. You don't show up, I'll send one of my ranch hands to get you. I mean it. You're coming." Willie patted Annabelle's arm. "I'm so glad you're back. You remember the way out to the ranch, don't you?"

She nodded, choked up. The last thing she wanted to do was have Thanksgiving at the ranch with her ex-almost-fiancé.

"Luke said something about them going huntin' so I'll need your help," Willie said, as if to let her know Dawson probably wouldn't be there. Apparently thinking it was all settled, Willie breezed off with a cart overflowing with food. She'd made it sound as if Annabelle showing up for Thanksgiving was doing *her* the favor. That was Willie.

But just the thought of one of Willie's meals made her stomach rumble. Also, she had no doubt that the woman would do exactly what she said she would, send a hired hand after her. So Annabelle knew she had no choice. She'd be back on the Rogers Ranch tomorrow for Thanksgiving—just like old times.

Except Dawson would be hunting with his brother instead of sitting next to her.

What had she just agreed to? Reaching into the bakery display, she grabbed a package of assorted donuts, one each of all her favorites. Now if she could just get out of this store without anyone else recognizing her.

MARY SUE HAD tried a half dozen times to reach her mother. When Carla answered, she recalled that her mother had gone shopping in Havre for the day.

"I just saw all your messages," her mother said. "What was so important that I had to call you the moment I got home?"

In the background she could hear that her mother was putting away groceries. "The old Clementine place. Have you ever been inside it?"

"No, why? I heard it's a mess and that Frannie collected everything under the sun. Is it in terrible shape inside?"

"Full to the brim, but there is something odd. On the plans from the county office, it shows that there was once an alcove off the kitchen."

"So, what is there now?" her mother asked as she worked.

"A wall."

Carla stopped putting away her groceries. "A wall?"

"It's as if there never was an alcove."

She heard her mother sit down heavily. "Why would someone close off an alcove?"

"That's what I want to know."

"You sure the planning office didn't give you the wrong house?"

"I'm sure. I even went back down there this afternoon and double-checked. There was definitely an alcove there about three wide by six feet long and eight foot high." Just large enough to hide a body. Or more bodies, if you stacked them, she thought, but didn't say.

"That is definitely odd," her mother agreed. "It shouldn't hurt the sale of the house, though. Annabelle is going to leave the wall, isn't she?"

"I got that impression. Still, it's kind of spooky, don't you think?"

"Oh, Mary Sue," her mother said, clearly hefting herself to her feet again. "Stop watching those zombie shows all the time. Why don't you come over and help me bake the pies? I'm dead on my feet."

Why not? "Do you need me to bring anything?"

Her mother had grown quiet, as if thinking about the question Mary Sue had asked her. But when she spoke it had nothing to do with Thanksgiving pies.

"You know, it didn't come out until she died, but Frannie never married."

"But I thought her husband died before she moved to Whitehorse?"

"But there'd been a man in her life, her son's father. So who was he?"

"Don't know. As far as I heard, Frannie never even dated, although Inez told me that she saw a man over there one time. Never saw him again."

Mary Sue was more interested in why Frannie had

closed up that alcove. "Maybe she killed the man and walled him up in the alcove."

"Oh, Mary Sue, Frannie wouldn't hurt a fly."

"That's what Annabelle said." But Mary Sue couldn't help but wonder what—or who—might be behind that wall. People often surprised you, especially the innocent-looking ones, she'd found.

# Chapter Five

Annabelle felt sick as she pulled into her driveway. She glanced over at the box of donuts on the passenger seat next to her. The box was almost empty. She hadn't even waited until she got home before she'd started in on them. Seeing Willie had upset her. It had brought back too many memories of Dawson. Too many memories in general.

She couldn't take her eyes off the remaining donuts, especially the last lemon-filled one. It had been years since she'd had a donut. Now that she had...

Hurriedly she slammed the lid closed on the ones that were left. Had she really thought she could sneak into town, sell the house, take care of her problems and slip out in the dead of night before anyone learned the truth?

"I'm such a fool," she said as she grabbed the donut box and the bag of food she'd ended up buying and exited her car. Earlier, she hadn't bothered locking the front door of the house and was glad now. Juggling everything, she managed to open the door and get inside without dropping the donut box.

Kicking the door closed behind her, she moved

through the dark house toward the kitchen. Moonlight fingered its way through the open blinds, painting the floor and walls with bands of light and dark. She was fumbling for the kitchen light switch when she thought she heard something.

Suddenly the hair stood up on the back of her neck. She felt her eyes widen in alarm as her gaze slowly shifted to the far side of the kitchen and that stupid wall that wasn't supposed to be there. Enough moonlight came through the window over the sink to throw a ghostly white haze over the dated kitchen.

But it was the dark spot that held her gaze. She stared at *the wall* as her heart began to hammer in her chest. There appeared to be a stain on the lower half of it. Dark like…blood, she could hear Mary Sue say, as if something had leaked through from the other side.

That was impossible after all these years. But still… Annabelle took a step back and bumped into the counter making her drop one of the bags of groceries and let out a stifled scream. The bag with the milk, orange juice and coffee hit the floor with a loud crash.

Still her eyes were on the spot with the stain. It had to be just a trick of the moonlight. Just a strange shadow. She groped for the light switch, anxious to prove that that was all it was.

She managed to put down the rest of the groceries and the donut box on the counter, all the time keeping an eye on the stain as if she thought it might grow. Or worse, begin to seep out onto the faded linoleum floor.

Pulling out her cell phone, she dialed her sister Chloe as she kept looking for the overhead light switch. "Why didn't you and TJ stay at the house?" she demanded the moment her sister answered.

"Annabelle? Are you drunk? What time is it?" Chloe sounded as if she'd been asleep.

She glanced at the clock. It was only ten. But ten in Montana was midnight back East. "You heard me. Why didn't you stay in Grandmother's house?"

"So it's Grandmother's house now? I thought it was yours? You're the one who inherited it, as you are fond of telling us."

"You're not answering my question." She moved cautiously along the counter until she reached the wall with the light switch—right where she now remembered it being. She snapped it on, blinded for a moment by the sudden light that filled the kitchen. The spot on the wall disappeared. Disappeared as if it had never been there at all.

Her relief made her go weak, even as she felt foolish. Of course it had been just a trick of the light and dark. A shadow. What had made her think blood? Mary Sue. She shivered, though, since she still had a wall where an alcove had once been.

"We didn't want to stay in the house." Her sister sounded defensive.

"Why?"

"Why do you care?" Chloe demanded. "We don't talk for months and this is what you have to say to me?"

"Was there something in the house that…unnerved you?" Annabelle forced herself to ask. Forced herself to admit that the house spooked her. She wanted to throttle Mary Sue for telling her about the missing alcove, about old ladies who killed people and buried them who knew where, about school kids avoiding the place on Halloween night after her grandmother had died because they saw her ghost in the window.

"What's going on, Annabelle?"

She shook her head, exhausted, dirty and donut sick. She hadn't called her sisters when she'd gotten in trouble because they'd had a fight over the house and weren't talking. But she also hadn't wanted to admit that her career was over and she was flat broke. So there hadn't been anyone close to her to confide in, since her circle of so-called friends already knew and had disappeared. Disappeared like the stain on the wall, leaving her scared and alone.

"It's nothing. Everything is fine," she said, remembering her sisters' reactions when they'd gotten the news about their grandmother's will. She was still hurt and angry about the snotty things they'd said—even if they'd been true.

"So, you've sold the house."

"Not yet, but soon. I'm sorry I bothered you." She disconnected and stood staring at the wall. Why would her grandmother close off the alcove? What if there had never been an alcove?

She swore that if Mary Sue showed up tomorrow and admitted she'd had the wrong set of house plans, Annabelle would throttle her.

# Chapter Six

"Did he get on a plane?" Bernie said into the phone as he pushed out of the wheelchair to the window.

"He did. I'm babysitting his cat."

"He has a cat?" Bernie realized how little he knew about his nephew, and yet he felt good about this errand he'd sent Robby on. This time he wasn't wrong. This time the woman really was Baby Doll. It surprised him that, more than getting back what she'd taken from him, he wanted to know why. Why she left him. Had it always only been about the money for her?

Bernie shook his gray head. He knew in his heart that couldn't be true. He'd loved her. Baby Doll had to have loved him. Robby had to find proof. Bernie couldn't die in peace until he knew.

"If you hear anything, let me know. I'm like on another planet in this place." As he disconnected, he happened to look down at his wastebasket. It hadn't been emptied, but the newspaper, the one from Whitehorse, Montana, was gone.

He was positive that he'd put it in the trash. But maybe he'd only thought about it. Getting old annoyed the devil out of him. His memory…it played tricks on him. He glanced around the room, sure the newspaper had to be here. Who would take the paper—with holes in it where he'd carefully, almost surgically removed sections?

His heart began to pound. The paper wasn't here. Realization settled in like crowbar to his gut. Someone had taken it from his wastebasket. He glanced toward the hall, thinking of his pretty, nice nurse. He shook his head. It hadn't been her. But he hadn't been paying close attention lately to new employees, new patients and their visitors, strangers on the property.

Damned if he wasn't getting old. He'd let his guard down, a mistake he would never have made when he was younger.

His legs suddenly felt weak. He moved to the wheelchair and dropped into it. His pulse thundered in his ears as he looked out toward the canal. Past it, he saw a boat moving slowly down the canal with two men in it and swore. Feds.

ANNABELLE WOKE AT daylight after a night of tossing and turning. The old bed sagged and groaned under her as she flung her feet over the side. Her head hurt and her stomach didn't feel all that great, either. But then again, that could have been the donuts.

After seeing what looked like a bloodstain on the wall in the kitchen and calling her sister, half in hysterics, she'd lost her appetite and gone straight to bed. Had she really eaten almost all of the donuts? Just the thought made her nauseous.

As she opened the bedroom door and padded across the hall to the bathroom, she couldn't shake off the weird dreams she'd had during the night. They seemed to float in and fade out like a weak radio station.

She shivered as she sat down on the cold toilet seat. One dream was more real than any of the other bits and pieces that kept coming back to her. Grandma Frannie had been standing at the end of her bed last night, looking so real and alive that Annabelle had been terrified. Worse, her grandmother had spoken to her.

*I know you wonder why I left the house only to you. I'm sorry, but you're the only one can handle it. You're the one most like me. Your sisters can't deal with the truth about what's behind that wall.*

Now Annabelle laughed with a shake of her head. It was obvious where that dream had come from. Mary Sue and all those crazy things she'd been saying.

Finishing her business, she padded back to the bedroom and pulled on the same dirty clothes as yesterday. She didn't see much reason to look for more ugly clothes to wear to clean out this place.

As she padded barefoot across the bedroom floor, one of the boards creaked loudly, reminding her of all the moaning and groaning the house had done last night. She didn't remember it being this bad when she was young. Or maybe that, too, had been part of the dream.

She took another step and felt the floorboard under her give a little. Looking down, she saw that the board appeared to be loose. Leaning closer, she made out a scratch mark at the end where it looked as if someone had used a screwdriver on it. To pry it up?

Kneeling down, she tried to work it free with her fingers. It moved enough that she had no doubt it would come loose—with a little help. In the kitchen she didn't locate a screwdriver, but she did find a butter knife.

Back in the bedroom, she knelt on the floor again and pried at the end where she'd noticed the scratches in the wood. The board popped up, bringing with it an old-house smell. She hesitated. There could be all kinds of creepy-crawly things under there.

Still, she carefully lifted the floorboard, aware of the spiderwebs stuck to it. Setting it aside, she cautiously peered down into the space below. Under the floorboards was another board. While the space was dusty and filled with cobwebs, she thought she saw something pushed back out of sight. Grimacing, she reached down and pulled out a battered metal box.

With a cleaning rag she'd been using yesterday, she removed the spiderwebs and dust on the box. Sitting down she pulled it between her legs and tried to open it. Locked.

She picked up the butter knife and had just gone to work on the lock when she heard the doorbell ring. As she looked out, she saw an old man standing out there. He wore a baseball cap on his short white hair. His coat was red-and-black checked wool, and he appeared to be wearing a dress shirt under it.

He rang the bell again. She thought about staying where she was behind the corner of the curtains until he went away, but he seemed determined as he rang the bell yet another time. He glanced toward her car and seemed ready to keep ringing until someone answered.

With a groan, Annabelle got to her feet. She stuck the box into one of the dresser drawers and went to the front door, patting at her hair as she went. Whatever the man was selling, she wasn't buying.

"Yes?" she asked briskly as she flung open the door. "I'm sorry but I'm really busy and—"

"You must be Annabelle," the man said as he smiled and leaned on his cane. She hadn't seen the cane from the window. Nor had she been able to see his face clearly. He looked to be in his late seventies or early eighties, though fit.

"You're just as your grandmother described you," he was saying.

It was worse than she'd originally thought. He wasn't just some random passerby. The slacks and dress shoes should have been a dead giveaway. Men in Whitehorse wore dressy boots and jeans to everything from a wedding to a funeral.

This man must be the pastor from the church her grandmother attended. Or a well-meaning member of the congregation who wanted to invite her to Sunday services.

"I'm sensing that your grandmother didn't tell you about me," the man said. "Where are my manners? I'm Lawrence Clarkston. Your grandmother's…boyfriend."

*"Boyfriend?"*

The man laughed. "Male companion?"

"You and grandmother…" She didn't know what to say. Frannie had a beau? After all these years? Clearly, he wasn't from around here. Something about the man made her nervous. He kept trying to see past her into the house. "I should get back to work."

"I can see that you're busy." He glanced over her shoulder again. "Packing up her things, huh? Looks like quite a job. I'd be happy to help. If I could just come in for a minute—"

"Thanks, but I have it."

"If you're sure," he said. "I'll come some other time." The man turned back toward the street, leaning heavily on his cane as he headed for a dark car parked at the curb, making her wonder how many secrets her grandmother had kept from her.

DAWSON TOOK OFF his Stetson to shoo the last of the cows back onto Rogers Ranch property before going to work on the fence. The sun was barely up, just hitting the tops of the Little Rockies. The November air was cold enough that he wished he were in front of his kitchen woodstove having another cup of coffee.

But he'd been awake for hours after a long night of tossing and turning. He didn't need to search for a reason for his unrest. Annabelle Clementine. That she'd haunted his dreams only made him more angry with himself. He'd thought he'd put that woman out of his life for good and now she showed up back in town?

He cursed under his breath as he pulled his chain saw from the bed of his truck and cranked it up. A tree had fallen and taken out a portion of his barbed-wire fence. He made short work of cutting up the tree and tossing the firewood into the back of the pickup. Sadie watched from inside the cab, barking at the cows that came over to see what was going on.

As he was loading the chain saw, his brother drove up. For a moment, he thought Luke had come to help. But then he noticed that Luke wasn't alone. His girlfriend, Sally, was with him, and his brother was clad in hunter orange and winter boots.

He wondered how much hunting Luke would get done with Sally along. No wonder his brother hadn't gotten his deer yet.

Dawson leaned against the side of his pickup as Luke approached, telling himself to keep that thought to himself. "I wondered what you were doing up so early," he said as his brother pulled alongside and whirred down his window.

"Mom said you were mending fence." Luke quickly lost interest, his gaze going to the Little Rockies. "Heard about a big buck that was seen on up the road. We thought we'd check it out." His baby brother's gaze finally lit on him again. "You look like hell. Rough night?" There was humor in his brother's tone as if enjoying the moment. Not that Luke wanted him to lose sleep over Annabelle Clementine's return. But Luke wouldn't mind seeing proof that his big brother cared more than he'd said he did.

"Just worried the cattle would get out with the fence down," Dawson said noncommittally. He might look like hell, but he wasn't about to admit who had kept him awake most of the night. "Some of us put work ahead of…" he shot Sally a look "…hunting."

"Uh-huh," Luke said, not taking the bait.

"I need to get this finished." Dawson pushed off the side of his pickup. "Good luck finding that big buck."

Had he really thought he could make his brother feel guilty enough to help him? Luke drove off toward the Little Rockies with a honk of his horn, a wave of his hand and a shouted, "Save me some turkey."

CLOSING THE FRONT door as Lawrence Clarkston left, Annabelle went back into the house and immediately resumed filling boxes. Her grandmother had a boyfriend? In all the years she'd lived with her grandmother, Frannie had steered clear of men, saying that her husband had been the love of her life. That there was no other man for her.

And then along comes Lawrence Clarkston? Annabelle tried to figure out why he'd made her nervous. Because he wasn't Frannie's type, she thought, frowning, as she carried the full box of junk out to the porch. But, then again, who *was* Frannie's type?

It wasn't until later, when Dawson's mother called to tell her again that she was depending on her to show up at the house at eleven forty-five, that Annabelle quit working and went into the bedroom to start getting ready.

As she entered, she saw the gaping hole where she'd removed the floorboard and now quickly replaced it. All she needed to do was step into that hole and break her leg. Seeing the hole, she remembered the metal box. The surprise of meeting Frannie's boyfriend had caused her to forget all about it.

She took the box out of the drawer and, butter knife

in hand, went to work on the lock. As she worked, she thought of Willie's call. She really couldn't be late. She hadn't planned on going out to the Rogers Ranch for Thanksgiving. Yesterday, even as she was nodding agreement, she was thinking of an excuse for when she would call her today to get out of it.

Now, though, she realized she had little choice but to show up. She knew the woman well enough to know that Willie didn't make idle threats. She would send someone after Annabelle. And what was the harm with Dawson and his brother out hunting? It wasn't like Willie was playing matchmaker, hoping to get her and Dawson back together.

Also, she remembered other Thanksgivings she'd shared at the Rogers Ranch. Willie put on a feast. Just the thought made her stomach growl. But she doubted Willie needed her help. She'd always admired Dawson's mom and had felt close to her. Maybe Willie felt the same. Why else would the woman forgive her for hurting her oldest son and invite her to Thanksgiving dinner?

The lock finally gave on the metal box. Putting down the butter knife, Annabelle carefully and slowly pried open the lid. Who had hidden this under the floorboards? The first people who owned the house? Or her grandmother? But if it had been Frannie, why hide a locked box under the floorboards?

The hinges groaned as the lid rose. An even mustier scent than the house rose from the metal box. She'd been worried about what she would find and was a little disappointed to see that the box was only filled with old photos and some yellowed newspaper clippings.

She picked up a few of the black-and-white photos, thumbed through them and realized that she didn't recognize any of the faces. Who knew how long they'd been under the house? She doubted they were even Frannie's, given the way the people in the photos were dressed. Either way, Annabelle didn't have time to go through them right now.

Hearing the coffeemaker shut off, she carried the box into the kitchen and absently put it on the table out of the way while she poured herself a cup of strong coffee before taking a shower and getting ready.

It had been years since she'd driven out to the Rogers Ranch, not that she could ever forget how to get there. It would feel strange being there, though. At least Dawson wouldn't be around, although she feared it was only a matter of time before he'd hear she was back. Or worse, that she'd run into him.

She couldn't help but wonder how much he'd changed in the past thirteen years. He could be bald with a potbelly. The thought made her laugh. She wondered if she would even recognize him.

WALKING INTO THE large ranch house on Thanksgiving Day, Dawson saw that the table was set for at least a dozen people. He shook his head, smiling. His mother. Around the holidays, she took in every stray who crossed her path.

"Nothing like offering people a decent meal," Willie would say. "It's a small thing, opening your kitchen to those who can use it." Every year, his mother found those who could use it and filled every seat, and then some, at their huge ranch-house table.

He followed the aroma of turkey and dressing, passing a dozen pies on the sideboard. How many people had she invited? He found Willie in the kitchen laughing with one of the neighbor ladies. His mother was in her element in this kitchen, her face glowing, her eyes bright.

"Well, look who's here!" Willie announced when she saw him and hurried over to give him a kiss on the cheek. She was a tall, lean woman with a warm face that was tanned year-round and seemed backlit with sunshine. Her smile had warmed more hearts than even he could imagine.

She'd had dozens of offers to remarry since Dawson's father had died, but she'd laughed them off, saying the last thing she needed was a husband. He often worried that she had turned down some good ones because she hadn't wanted to install a stepfather for her sons.

His mother motioned to the other women in the kitchen. "You know Kay from down the road," she said, indicating a gray-haired woman in her seventies. "And Patricia." The fiftysomething spinster who belonged to his mother's church nodded at him. Whitehorse, as small as it was, had a half dozen churches—and as many bars.

He smiled. "Yes, Mother, I've known Kay since I was two. Hello, Mrs. Welch. And I've known Patricia for only half my life."

His mother laughed. "And I guess I don't have to

introduce you to this woman," she said as Annabelle Clementine came out of the pantry holding a huge bowl of cranberry relish. "I believe you've known her since you were...ten."

"Seven," he corrected as his gaze met Annabelle's. She looked as startled as he was to see *her.* Had she thought he wouldn't be here? "She was five."

She wore the black outfit that he'd seen her in by the river just the day before. She looked sexy as hell, but then, she'd looked good even in the sweatshirt and baggy jeans she'd been cleaning in yesterday.

"Seven," his mother repeated. "My mistake. Just put that on the table," she said to Annabelle. "Dawson, you can take this out." She reached into the refrigerator and handed him several plates with sticks of butter on them.

He shot her a Mother-how-could-you? look.

She gave him an impatient look back. "I was delighted to learn that Annabelle was back in town. I'm just happy she could join us for Thanksgiving dinner." His mother cocked her head and narrowed her eyes as if to say, *You'd better be polite, or else*, and then shooed him out to the dining room. No son of Wilhelmina Rogers would dream of being impolite to a guest at her house.

He followed Annabelle out to the dining room and out of earshot of his mother. "What are you doing here?" he asked under his breath.

"What are *you* doing here? I thought you'd be hunting."

"I was. Until *yesterday.*" He waited for her to say something about their meeting on the highway. When she didn't, he added, "Which was a good thing or you could still be sitting beside the road in your fancy silver sports car without a drop of gas."

Her eyes widened in alarm and her cheeks flushed. "That was...*you*?"

He let out a bitter laugh. "How easily she forgets."

## Chapter Seven

Those golden-brown eyes. She felt a shiver. How could she not have recognized him? She hadn't gotten a good look at him, not that she'd been trying. The cowboy had looked so...scruffy, so filthy, so rough.

She groaned inwardly and lied, since she would have run out of gas not a half mile up the road if he hadn't helped her. "I wouldn't have stopped if I'd known it was you."

"Thanks."

"No, what I meant was..."

"Don't worry, I got the message." His gaze locked with hers. "Just like I got it thirteen years ago."

"Dawson—" She stopped. Just saying his name was a painful reminder of the intimacy they'd shared—and she'd thrown away. "I never—"

"Please don't."

No matter what she said, there was no way she could take it all back. She looked into those warm brown eyes, now so familiar in that handsome face. He was clean-shaven today, accentuating the razor edge of his unyielding jaw. Dawson looked damned good. The

Western shirt he wore stretched over the taut muscles of his wide shoulders. She didn't need to see his abs to know they would be rock hard and still tanned from a summer spent bare chested on the ranch.

She swallowed, remembering the feel of his body against hers. "I'm sorry. I should have at least offered to pay you something for the gas."

*"Seriously?"* He looked even more disappointed in her. "Girl, you've been livin' in the big city for too long," he said with a shake of his head. "Out here in this part of Montana we help each other without expecting anything in return. I thought maybe you might have remembered that from growing up here, but then again, you couldn't wait to get out of here, could you? What was it you said to me? Unlike me, you were going to make something of yourself."

She felt her cheeks flame again. "Daw—"

"Don't bother. You were real clear when you left town. You didn't stutter," he said and turned on his boot heel to stride off, all long legs and attitude.

She watched him go, swamped with a wave of regret that she hadn't expected. For years she'd told herself that she hadn't left behind anything in Whitehorse. She hadn't even come back for her grandmother's funeral. What kind of woman was she?

"I understand that you need to spread your wings, Annabelle," Grandma Frannie had said the day she'd packed to leave. "There's nothing for you here. You need space to find what it is you're looking for. I was just like you when I was your age. I wanted to take a big bite out of the world. I craved it so much, it was eating me up inside. Fame, fortune, whatever it is, I know if anyone can find it, it will be you. I just hope it's everything you expect it to be."

"But I hate to leave you."

"Don't be ridiculous. It's time for this little bird to fly the nest." She'd hugged Annabelle. "I have great hopes for you no matter what happens."

"That's because I'm your favorite."

Frannie had laughed. "You're the one, all right," she'd said with a wink. "You're the one I'm depending on in the end."

Annabelle realized now that Patricia had come into the dining room and said something to her. "I'm sorry. My mind was a million miles away."

"I gathered that," the woman said. "I was saying that I hadn't realized you and Dawson had a history. Willie was just telling me that she always thought you'd be her daughter-in-law."

There was that pain again. She'd left this life behind without a backward glance and yet… She thought of the tree house two doors down from her grandmother's and the first time she'd laid eyes on Dawson. Being the way she'd always been, she had climbed up the ladder to the tree house even though she could read the sign: Do Not Enter. She'd been reading since she was three.

Earlier, she'd sneaked away from her sisters. They'd been told not to let her leave the yard, but they often got to playing with their dolls and not paying any attention to her.

Once up in the tree house, she hadn't been able to get down. She'd been five. "Precocious for your age," is what Frannie always said. "A brat," is what her older sisters contended.

Seven-year-old Dawson had come along and seen her up there. "Get down from there right now!" he'd ordered. "The sign says—"

"I know what the sign says," she'd said, surprised by how scared she was about being this high off the ground. Her words had come out in a stutter.

"What's your name?" he'd asked as he started up the ladder.

She'd watched him, feeling sick to her stomach and wishing she hadn't looked down. She tried to say her name but it came out "Anna."

"All right, Annie, you just have to trust me, okay?" He had been almost to her by then. He was nice, nothing like those boys her sisters made goggle eyes over.

Instinctively, she had trusted him. She'd let him help her down from the tree house, saving her. Just like he'd saved her on the highway yesterday.

"We used to play together as kids, that's all," she said to Pamela now, feeling the pinch of the lie. Dawson had always been there for her when she'd needed him. But while his feet had been firmly planted in this county's soil, hers had itched to kick the dust off her shoes and put this town in her rearview mirror. Too bad it hadn't turned out quite like she'd planned it.

"You look like a woman who could use a drink," said a male voice behind her. She turned to see Dawson's best friend, Jason Reynolds. "Welcome back to Whitehorse."

She felt a surge of relief. "I can't tell you how great it

is to see a friendly face." Jason had always been nice to her and was one of the few people who had seemed to understand her need to leave Whitehorse—and Dawson.

He laughed now and hugged her. "I heard you were back, but I didn't believe it."

"Just long enough to sell my grandmother's house."

"Oh," he said and glanced toward the kitchen where Dawson was leaning against the counter scowling. "That explains a lot, then. What do you say when we're done here today we meet at the Mint Bar?"

She hesitated, but only for a moment. "One drink. I have a lot of work to do, but you're on."

DAWSON DID HIS best to be civil during the meal, but having Annabelle there just like old times had ruined his appetite. His mother had acted as if his high school girlfriend was part of the family.

"Jason flirted with her the entire meal," Dawson snapped after he and his brother had helped take dishes to the kitchen. Their mother had shooed them out to the family room where there was a game on the television. Jason had left right after the meal, saying he had to stop by the nursing home to see his grandmother. Annabelle had cut out shortly after that when their mother wouldn't let her help with the dishes.

His brother now grinned from the couch. His girlfriend, Sally, was having Thanksgiving with her own family. Willie and an assortment of guests were in the kitchen, finishing up. "It's your own fault. You're the one who gave Jason your seat next to Annabelle. Looked like the two of them were having a fine time."

Dawson growled under his breath. He hadn't missed a moment of it. "It wasn't my idea, having her over for Thanksgiving. It was Mother's. All I need is Willie playing matchmaker."

Luke laughed. "Well, if it makes you feel any better, Mom wasn't all that happy that Jason and Annabelle hit it off at dinner."

Dawson got to his feet, unable to sit another moment. "Oh, come on. What's the harm if Jason flirted with her? Like you said, she isn't staying. So lighten up. Anyway, once she gets her grandmother's house sold, she'll be gone."

"Just not soon enough."

"I thought you were over her?" Luke said. "That you didn't care she was back. That—where are you headed?"

"I need a stiff drink."

"I think Mom's got some brandy that she uses for her fruitcakes. I know where she hides it."

Dawson shook his head. "I need to get out of here. Want to go to the Mint?"

THE MOMENT HE and his brother walked in, Dawson spotted Annabelle and almost turned back around and left. He would have if his brother hadn't stopped him.

"You can't keep dodging her," Luke argued. "You two are going to see each other. If you really don't care, then what's the big deal?"

He knew he was being manipulated, but he wanted a drink more than he wanted to argue with his brother. The band was finishing up a cheating song. Just the sight of Annabelle there with Jason... He was moving toward the bar when Jason saw him and called him over to their table.

"Everything all right?" his friend asked. Dawson ordered a shot of whiskey and a beer from the waitress who appeared.

"Why wouldn't everything be all right?" he snapped as he looked at Annabelle. She was pretending interest in the couples out on the dance floor.

"Your mama outdid herself on that Thanksgiving dinner," Jason said, as if ignoring the tension at the table.

"You should know. You've been showing up there every year since we were kids."

His friend smiled. "Got up on the wrong side of the bed, did you?"

Dawson glared at him, feeling like a jackass. Jason was his best friend and part of the Rogers family. The waitress brought his drinks. He picked up the shot of whiskey, downed it and chased it with some of the beer. As the band wrapped up their song and broke into a slow one, he turned to Annabelle.

"Let's dance," he said and reached for her hand.

She hesitated, but he caught her fingers and pulled her up from her seat and out on the dance floor. "Dawson, what are you doing?" she demanded once they were away from the table.

"Dancing." He leaned closer, caught a whiff of her perfume and felt his head spin. Did she still wear his favorite? Or had she just put it on for the dinner, thinking he'd be there? Or had she known Jason would be there? Hadn't she said she thought Dawson would be out hunting?

He hated being jealous, but he couldn't seem to help himself. "Don't you think you at least owe me a dance?"

"For the gas?"

He shook his head as they began to move to the music. "One dance for breaking my heart. It's a cheap deal at twice the price."

ANNABELLE COULD HEAR the hurt in his voice, the anger and something she couldn't put her finger on. They hadn't spoken at dinner after that short discussion in the dining room before the turkey was served. But she'd felt him watching her throughout the meal.

"I broke your heart?" she asked, wondering if that was true. He'd been furious, that much she'd known. And hurt. But he hadn't even bothered to stop by the day she'd left. Nor had she heard from him since.

"What do you think?" He locked eyes with her.

She felt them drilling into her. Surprisingly, as angry as he was, it felt intimate. She swallowed and looked away, thinking he'd given up pretty easily when she'd said she was leaving town. "If that's true, I'm sorry."

"Don't be. You proved that leaving was your best choice. If you'd stayed here and married me…well, as you said, you weren't cut out to be a Montana ranch-woman. Clearly you made the right choice."

Her smile hurt her. "I didn't think I had a choice back then. It felt like leaving was something I had to do."

"And look how it turned out."

"Yes." She glanced away, her eyes burning with tears. Yes, look how it had turned out. "It hasn't been easy."

"But then, no one is stronger or more determined than you are."

He made that sound like a compliment. She looked into his handsome face. Those warm brown eyes had always been her downfall. "Whether you believe it or not, it wasn't easy to leave you."

Dawson laughed. "Oh, you didn't seem to have that much trouble doing it." He brushed a lock of her hair back from her forehead. His fingertips felt hot against her sensitive skin. She trembled even though it was warm on the dance floor. Dawson's hand on her waist seemed to burn the tender flesh under her blouse.

She looked into those eyes and remembered all of it—from their first kiss to the last time they'd made love. Leaving him was the hardest thing she'd ever done. She hadn't wanted him to make it easy. Had she wanted him to fight for her? To beg her to stay? Well, he hadn't. He'd let her go and walked away.

Not that she would have stayed, she told herself. But they would never know, would they? "Dawson." The slow country song was coming to an end. His gaze shifted to her lips and she knew he was going to kiss her. The ache at her center intensified as he brushed his mouth over hers. "Dawson," she breathed.

His arms tightened around her and she was drawn into his rock-hard body. Her lips parted as his mouth took possession of hers.

Had the song not died away, she could have stayed right there in his arms, captured in the elixir of that kiss.

But the music stopped and so did the kiss. She looked at the handsome cowboy and felt the full weight of the lie she was living. If he only knew how she'd traded him for a life she'd thought she wanted more than her next breath only to fail so miserably—

She stepped out of his arms, saw the hurt and experienced a loss like none she had ever felt before. She couldn't hurt this man again. But walking away from him broke her heart one more time. She'd compared every man she'd met in the past thirteen years to Dawson—and they'd all come up lacking.

She tore herself away and headed for the door. She was almost there when someone grabbed her arm. She turned, thinking it would be Dawson. It was Jason.

"Dawson just left by the back way," he said, drawing her back to the table. "One drink," he reminded her. "It will give Dawson a chance to make a clean getaway and I think he needs that right now."

Annabelle felt unsteady on her feet as she let him lead her back to the table. The last thing she wanted was a drink. But she couldn't bear running into Dawson in the parking lot. Tears burned her eyes. She touched the tip of her tongue to her lower lip. Her mouth still tingled from his kiss. She bit down on her lip and tried not to cry.

"I should never have come back here," she said, picking up the drink Jason pushed in front of her as they sat down.

"It will get easier," he told her.

She shook her head. "I'm not staying that long. Once I get that house cleaned out…" The magnitude of what she still had to do overwhelmed her. The band was taking a break but had punched in some songs on the jukebox.

"I can't let you hurt Dawson again," Jason said, taking her by surprise. "He was a mess for a long time after you left. I'm not sure he's tough enough to go through that again."

She realized that he'd seen her and Dawson kissing. "He's the one who made me dance with him and the kiss…" She was going to say it was all Dawson, but that would have been another lie.

"It's taken him years to get over you. You hurt him bad," Jason said, not unkindly. "He spent months saving up for that engagement ring."

Wanting to disappear under the table, she took a gulp of her drink. It tasted bitter on her tongue and it felt as if she was trying to wash away the memory of the kiss. Another lie. She wanted to take that kiss to her grave.

"I'm only telling you this because he's my friend and so are you," Jason was saying. "I really thought you'd come back. You know, that day you left, I thought you'd realize what you were giving up. But then I saw your photograph on a billboard down in Denver a year later. I said, 'Wow, I used to know that girl.' You really showed Dawson. Hell, you showed everyone in town."

She felt like crying. "I didn't show anyone anything," she said under her breath. "Don't worry. I'm leaving just as soon as I can. In the meantime, I will stay as far away from Dawson as possible, and I'm sure he feels the same way." She pushed the remainder of the drink away. Alcohol was the last thing she needed. "I have to go. Thank you. For the drink. For…" She reached for his hand and squeezed it. "For the advice." For telling her that she'd broken Dawson's heart and warning her not to do it again?

"I don't want to see you hurt, either," Jason said. "Dawson is never leaving Montana. He's a cowboy. He'd die in California."

She nodded. "I know." Why hadn't she just let Mary Sue sell the house and send her the money? Why had she come back here?

DAWSON LEFT THE BAR, needing fresh air and distance. He should never have danced with Annabelle—let alone kissed her. He was mentally kicking himself for that impulsive moment of weakness when he noticed her fancy sports car. What called his attention to the vehicle was the man hooking it to a wrecker.

As he walked closer, he realized he didn't recognize the towing company. Nor had there seemed to be anything wrong with Annabelle's car. Other than running out of gas. That couldn't be the problem, since he'd given her almost a full tank.

"Hey," he said as he approached. "Why are you towing that car?"

"Stay out of it," the man said. "Just doing my job. I don't want any trouble. I have the paperwork right here." He reached into his jacket pocket and pulled out some folded sheets of paper.

Paperwork? "I know the woman who owns that car. I want to see those," Dawson said.

The man sighed, but stepped to him, unfolded the papers and handed them to him.

Reading under the streetlight, Dawson couldn't believe what he was seeing. *Her car was being repossessed for lack of payment?* He looked toward the bar, then at the wrecker operator. "There must be some mistake. Do you know who Annabelle Clementine is?"

"No mistake. She's a deadbeat like any other deadbeat."

He bristled at the man's words. "Look…" He glanced at the name on the paperwork: Chet's Retrieval Service. "Look, Chet. Come on, give the lady a break."

Chet gave Dawson an impatient look. "She's been given all kinds of breaks and now I had to come all this way to get the car. She's used up all her breaks."

"What does she owe?"

Chet kept hooking up the car.

"Just give me the amount." He withdrew a loose check from his wallet. "You have a pen?"

The wrecker operator stopped to look at him for a long moment, then sighed and took the papers from his hand, thumbed through them to a page and pointed at a figure at the bottom.

The amount took Dawson's breath away. How could she have gotten so far behind in her car payments? What had she been thinking, buying such an expensive car to begin with if she couldn't afford it?

The wrecker operator grinned, seeing Dawson's surprise. "Still want to bail her out?"

"Yes." He ground his teeth as he wrote the check for the full amount and handed to it him. "Unhook it."

The wrecker operator looked at the check. "I'm staying in town at the motel and cashing this first thing in the morning. If this bounces—"

"It isn't going to bounce," Dawson said indignantly. "Unhook it."

"I'll be going to your bank as soon as it opens in the morning. Don't make me have to look for this car again."

"I'll transfer the funds tonight online to my checking account. Don't worry. The owner of this car isn't going anywhere, anyway." He doubted she could afford money for gas to leave town right now. Things were beginning to make sense. Like the reason she was so anxious to get her grandmother's house sold. Why she was packing it up by herself, instead of hiring help. Why he'd seen her in the same outfit twice.

"But we keep this between us," Dawson added.

Chet gave him a pitying look as if he was the biggest sucker he'd ever met. "It's your money." The man folded the check, pocketed it and began to unhook Annabelle's car.

From behind him he heard a door slam, then a plaintive wail. "Wait!"

Dawson groaned as he turned to see Annabelle come out of the bar. She saw him, eyes narrowing as she stormed toward them.

ANNABELLE WAS IN the middle of her worst nightmare. At first, all she'd seen was her car dangling from the back of the wrecker. After months of avoiding the repo man, he'd caught up with her. She ran across the parking lot, telling herself she had to talk him out of taking her car. She needed it desperately if she hoped to get her grandmother's house sold.

What she hadn't seen at first was Dawson standing in the shadows. When he turned, her heart had dropped like a sack of potatoes. Instantly, she went on the defensive, since that was all she had. That and her badly damaged pride.

"What's going on?" she demanded, hands on her not-so-slim hips.

"I took care of it," Dawson said.

Annabelle looked from him to the wrecker driver who only gave her a satisfied grin and a shrug. She realized what had happened and felt her face burn with shame followed quickly by anger.

"How dare you?" she snapped, turning on Dawson. "How dare you take it upon yourself to pay my bills?"

Dawson pulled off his Stetson and raked a hand through his hair. "I couldn't let him take your car."

"It was none of your business."

"You're right." He put his hat back on and held up both hands in surrender. "I thought I was helping, but clearly…" He cursed under his breath before she swung back around on the repo man.

"This is just a misunderstanding between me and my bank. I will take care of it."

"Sure it is." The wrecker operator nodded with a grin that made her want to retch. "Out of my hands now. Take it up with…" he glanced toward Dawson "…your…friend."

She swung back around to find Dawson studying his

boots. Tears burned her eyes but she willed herself not to cry. Just when she'd thought things couldn't get any worse. She didn't have to look into Dawson's brown-eyed gaze to see the truth. He knew.

On top of that, he'd just saved her again. She thought she would die of embarrassment. If only the parking lot pavement would open up and swallow her.

"This must give you a lot of satisfaction," she said, biting off each word.

He glanced up, looking confused.

"I was so full of myself, leaving here to go make something of my life."

"You did what you set out to do."

She shook her head fighting tears. "Only to fail and come back here broke and—" The words caught in her throat as it constricted.

As the wrecker drove off, Dawson closed the distance between them, taking her shoulders in his hands. "You didn't fail."

She let out a strangled laugh and had to look away. "I got fired. Worse, blackballed. I'll never be able to get another modeling job."

"So?"

*"So?"* she demanded returning her gaze to him. "It's the only thing I know how to do, the only thing I ever planned to do."

"Plans change. I know you. You can do anything you set our mind to."

"Right."

"Don't sell yourself short. You just need a new plan."

She wiped at her tears. "Why are you being so nice to me?"

He released her shoulders. "Why wouldn't I be?"

*"Seriously?"*

"I was angry for a while, I'll admit it." His voice softened. "I was devastated when you left. But you were right. You needed to go off and follow your dream. And, Annie, you did it."

She heard what sounded like pride in his voice. And he'd called her Annie, his pet name for her.

"So it didn't work out quite like you thought it would. So what?"

So what? She looked away as she tried to swallow the lump in her throat.

"You were right about me, as well. I'm just a cowboy. I'm never going to set the world on fire. I'm happy chasing cows, mending fence, working on my old tractor."

She felt chagrin heat her face as she remembered saying he would be working on some old tractor the rest of his life. "I'm sorry for the awful things I said to you."

"Hell, girl, it forced me to buy a new tractor." He grinned and shrugged. "But I also got the old one running, as well."

She couldn't help but smile at him. "I'm glad you haven't changed. I'm even glad Whitehorse hasn't changed."

"That's only because you'll be selling your grandmother's house and leaving this one-horse town on your next adventure." He smiled when he said it, but the words still stung because she remembered saying them to Mary Sue. It had all been bravado and she felt ashamed.

What if she didn't want to leave? What was there for her here if she stayed? Those were the words she wanted to say, but they were stuck in her throat.

She opened her mouth, aching for the feel of his arms around her, and closed it again. When she finally spoke, her voice broke. "I will pay you back every dime." With that she turned, and with as much dignity as she could muster, walked to her car and drove away.

Back at the house, she stood for a moment just inside the door. She didn't want to go into the kitchen. She didn't want to see the blood spot on the wall where there might or might not have been an alcove.

But she needed a drink of water. Forcing herself to go into the kitchen, she quickly snapped on the light before glancing toward the wall. A laugh escaped her.

She was exhausted from packing boxes, from worry. From trying to ignore Dawson. From fighting emotions that seemed to overwhelm her at every turn. From living a lie.

But as she stood there, she remembered. There *had* been an alcove there growing up. The reason she hadn't remembered was because her grandmother had kept a hutch there that had filled up the space.

Why hadn't she remembered the hutch? Because it had been covered with knickknacks, plants, newspapers. Her grandmother had always been a collector. A hoarder.

So, when had Frannie gotten rid of the hutch? And why? Why close up that space? It made no sense. She shuddered. Was it possible there was something behind that wall? But what?

"This is silly," she said to the empty room. Anyone who knew grandmother wouldn't suspect her of...of what?

She hugged herself, blaming the crazy thoughts on her exhaustion. Sleep, that's what she needed. Tomorrow everything would look brighter. That made her laugh again because she knew better. Tomorrow she would again be faced with filling boxes and lugging them out to the porch. After that—

Determined not to think about it, she turned off the kitchen light but stood for a moment longer staring at the wall. No dark shadow resembling blood appeared. That was at least something.

ROB STARED OUT at the wide-open spaces in his headlights feeling nervous. It was so isolated out here in the middle of Montana. He hadn't seen another set of headlights for miles on the two-lane highway and that after flying for hours. It was next to impossible to get a decent flight from Florida to Montana—on Thanksgiving Day, no less. He'd been on four different planes, endured hours of layovers and had barely made the connection for the last one. Tired and irritable, he couldn't have felt worse about this so-called job.

Now he wasn't sure he was even on the right road. The rental car had a navigation system, but he hated those things. The rental agent had given him a paper map that now lay on the passenger seat.

According to the map, he just kept going north. If he hit Canada, well, then he'd gone too far. He hoped to find a town, a gas station, someplace he could stop and ask. But he'd driven miles without seeing a soul. Lots of cows, but little else.

Finally, as the sun was coming up, he spotted a gas station ahead and what was reportedly the town of Grass Range though he didn't see much town. He pulled in, bought gas, asked for directions.

"Just keep going up the road. Can't miss White-horse," the clerk told him after taking his money.

"Tell me it's bigger than this burg," Rob said.

The clerk, a young woman with red hair and freckles, laughed. "It's bigger."

"There a motel in Whitehorse?"

"Four, I think."

Four? Well, that was better than none, he thought as he climbed back into the rental car. He'd bought some large cookies, two peanut butter and two chocolate chip. He chased them down with a liter of cola as he drove.

He couldn't wait to get to Whitehorse, find out that the dead woman wasn't Bernie's Baby Doll, then head home. He'd missed Thanksgiving, not that he'd ever liked turkey.

As he drove, the country became wilder and more forbidding. He thought about Baby Doll, the woman who'd fooled the family kingpin, the great Bernard "Bernie the Hawk" McDougal.

Was it possible she had been hiding out all these years in this Wild West–looking country? Not the broad the family had described to him. She'd been one cagey woman. Rob couldn't see her way out here in Montana. If he could prove that this Francesca Marie Clementine wasn't Baby Doll, he would be on the first plane out of here.

He relaxed a little, turning on the radio and searching for a station. He found only one. "Shit-kicking music," his friend Murph would have called it. Normally, the two of them did the jobs together. It had surprised Rob when his uncle had wanted him to handle this one alone. Bernie really did think this old chick had been Baby Doll, which also meant he believed that she'd held on to the loot.

Yep, his uncle had to be losing it.

He decided to listen to the country music station. "When in Montana," Rob said as he watched the rental car eat up the miles of rolling ranch land, rugged river bottom and, finally, open prairie.

By the time he reached the outskirts of Whitehorse, he was tired enough that all he wanted to do was find a motel and get some sleep. But he knew his uncle would be calling, wanting an update.

The Grass Range convenience store clerk had been right about one thing. This town was a little bigger. But not much. Which made it almost too easy to find the Clementine place.

## *Chapter Eight*

Annabelle woke to daylight, blinked and covered her head with the duvet at the memory of the night before. Dawson knew everything now about her dire straits. Worse, he'd paid for her car not to be towed. She couldn't have been more mortified.

Even worse than that, she couldn't spend the day under the covers hiding out. She had to get up. This house had to be emptied out before she could sell it. Just the thought of another day loading junk into boxes made her groan. How could this now be her life?

That was a question she didn't want to contemplate. She'd rather fill boxes and lug them out to the porch, she thought as she threw back the covers and got out of bed. Feeling sorry for herself wasn't going to get her anywhere.

Last night she'd hated to face coming back to this place. It was much creepier after dark, especially with a breeze in the bare limbs of the cottonwoods and the pine boughs. The house had creaked and groaned more than the first night.

She started toward the kitchen to make coffee.

She wouldn't have a car if it wasn't for Dawson. She wouldn't even have made it to Whitehorse if he hadn't given her fuel. Tears welled in her eyes. She quickly wiped them away with the back of her hand, ashamed of the way she'd been acting. She'd yelled at Dawson for keeping her car from being towed. She'd just been so embarrassed. Maybe pushing people away was her one true talent, she thought as she stepped into the kitchen and got the coffee going.

She tried to think of what needed to be done this morning instead of mentally beating herself up. She needed to make another box run and then get back to work. Pouring herself a cup of coffee, she wandered into the living room and stood looking everything that remained. She felt overwhelmed. Not even the coffee helped.

But if she was anything, it was determined. She lifted her chin, telling herself she could do this. Like she had a choice. Finishing her coffee, she returned her cup to the kitchen then went to get dressed in her "work" clothes.

She reminded herself how hard it had been to succeed in the modeling business. Not discounting luck, she'd worked hard to get where she'd been. *Where she'd been.* It still hurt to think that she'd thrown it all away.

Shaking her head to dislodge those thoughts, she went to work, determined to put Dawson out of her mind. But it was so like Dawson to bail her out. Of course he'd want to know why. It had been a perfect opportunity to say *I told you so*.

But he hadn't. If anything he'd been kind. *Too kind.*

She grumbled under her breath. She didn't need his pity. She didn't need anyone's pity.

The thought of her dire circumstances—and worse, that Dawson knew—turned her stomach. This was what she'd hoped to avoid. She'd left this town so smug, so sure of herself, so determined to be someone... Now it made her laugh. She was a joke, and the only man she'd ever loved now knew it.

The knock at the door made her jump. For a moment, she thought it would be Dawson, as if just thinking about him had conjured him up.

But it was a pinch-faced little old gray-haired woman who was now peering in the window. She had her hands cupped around her watery eyes and her nose pressed to the glass.

"Can I help you?" Annabelle demanded, opening the door.

"There was a man looking in your windows last night," the woman said. "I live right next door and I looked out—"

"Mrs. Gilbert?" It had been years since she'd seen her grandmother's nosey neighbor.

"You're the trouble one, right?"

"Trouble one?" she echoed.

"The granddaughter Frannie worried about all the time."

"That would be me," she said—as her grandmother would have insisted, owning it.

"I ran him off. The man who was peeking in your windows. Might want to keep your blinds drawn. Those types often come back," Inez Gilbert said as she turned, cane in hand.

Seeing the cane reminded her of the man who'd stopped by yesterday morning. "Did my grandmother have a boyfriend?"

The elderly woman stopped to peer back at her.

"A distinguished-looking man who carries a cane? Said his name was Lawrence Clarkston."

"I saw him. Yesterday morning at your door," Inez said. "Never seen him before in my life. Nor was it him last night."

"So Frannie didn't—"

"She did not," her neighbor said, as she wobbled down the stairs and took off down the sidewalk. "If she had, I would have known."

"I'm sure you would have," Annabelle said under her breath.

Going back inside, she hugged herself. So, who was the man pretending to be her grandmother's boyfriend? Maybe more scary, who was the man Inez had seen peering in her windows last night?

Catching her reflection and the hideous outfit she was wearing, Annabelle promised herself she would go uptown and buy herself a pair of jeans and a couple of T-shirts.

In the meantime… She looked at the mess—not just in the house but in her life and burst into tears.

DAWSON DIDN'T THINK he had slept a wink. Not long after the sun rose, he drove over to the main ranch house to find his mother and brother in the kitchen.

"Rough night?" his mother asked and handed him a cup of coffee. "I could make you some breakfast."

He shook his head. "Thanks, but I'm not hungry."

"Well, something's gotten under your hide." She motioned to a chair at the table.

He hesitated, even though he knew the reason he'd driven over here so early in the morning was that he needed to talk to her. She'd been his sounding board since he was a kid. Nothing had changed. He glanced at his younger brother already sitting at the table.

"You want me to leave?" Luke asked, pretending to be insulted. "Hell, we both know what's bothering you."

"Language," their mother said as Luke shoved back his chair and started to get up.

"You can stay," Dawson said with a sigh, and his brother dropped back down, grinning. "But not a word of this leaves this room. Agreed?"

Luke nodded. His mother didn't bother. She knew how to keep a secret better than anyone he knew.

Without preamble, he said, "Annabelle's broke. That's why she's back."

His brother laughed. "Annabelle Clementine? What are you talking about? She was just on the cover of one of those fancy women's magazines."

"You read fancy women's magazines?" his mother asked.

Luke's face reddened. "I saw it at Sally's house." He turned to his brother. "This sounds like you just being jealous again, big brother. She left and made something of herself and you stayed here. You've always resented being forced to stay behind to take care of the ranch.

Now you're taking it out on her. Why don't you admit it? You're still hung up on her."

"I was wrong. I should have let you leave," Dawson said.

"Your brother means well." Their mother sent a withering look at Luke. "What do you mean, broke?"

"Flat broke." He told her about crossing paths with Annabelle south of town by the river.

"You didn't tell me that," Luke said.

Ignoring him, Dawson continued, "Last night at the bar, her car was almost repossessed. Apparently she hasn't been making her car payment for months." He didn't mention that Annabelle had been wearing the same outfit he'd first seen her in again yesterday at Thanksgiving dinner.

Willie shook her head. "Oh, the poor dear. Something must have happened. You have no idea what?"

"No, but it seems the only reason she's back is to sell her grandmother's house as quickly as possible to get herself out of trouble financially," he said. "More than likely she got in over her head with her supermodel lifestyle." He hated the bitterness he heard in his tone.

"What are you going to do about it?" his mother asked.

Dawson frowned and held up his hands. "Do about it? I gave her gas, I paid to keep her car from being repossessed—at least temporarily, and she told me to stay out of her business."

"She must be so embarrassed," Willie said. "You're the last person she'd want bailing her out."

"Exactly," he said.

"Well, there's a simple solution," Luke said, looking pleased with himself. "Sounds like it will take a while for her to get the house ready to sell, since it's packed with junk that has to be hauled to the dump. Also, Mary Sue doesn't think it will sell fast, especially this close to Christmas. There's time to tell her how you feel."

Dawson groaned. "If I did still have feelings for her, which I don't, what would be the point? I'm a Montana rancher. She's…whatever it is she is. There's a reason we broke up all those years ago. Not to mention that once she has money again, she'll be gone. She isn't interested in Montana or me. The sooner she gets out of town, the better." He finished his coffee and stood.

"Well, if that's the case," his mother said, "then you need to help her."

He stopped in his tracks. "What?"

"You want her out of town? She wants out of town. The solution is right in front of you. Help her get the house ready to sell. Otherwise, who knows how long she'll be around, running out of money."

Dawson stared at his mother. "If this is you match-making—"

"Not at all," Willie assured him. "I can see how Annabelle being in town is upsetting you—not to mention costing you money. Help her get the house sold, and if you're right, she'll be gone."

He eyed her suspiciously for a long moment, hating to admit that she might have a point. "Fine. But little brother, you're going to help. Bring the flatbed truck to Annabelle's this afternoon along with some of your friends. We're going to make a trip to the dump."

"Hey, don't involve me in this," Luke complained. "My solution requires a lot less lifting. Also I'm helping the neighbor this morning with his fence."

"Two this afternoon," Dawson said pointing a finger at his brother. "You're the one who is so interested in Annabelle…" He slammed out of the house, letting the door bang behind him.

"Help your brother," Willie said as she rose to get more coffee.

"There's no help for him. He's in love and too stubborn to admit it, as if you didn't know that when you invited Annabelle to Thanksgiving dinner."

Willie looked after her oldest son who was now driving away. "Did he only stay because he thinks I need him to help run the ranch?"

"No, Mom," Luke said, putting an arm around her shoulder. "I was just giving him a hard time. He's a born Montana cowboy and rancher. He's just mad because he didn't put up more of a fight thirteen years ago."

"I'm not sure it would have helped," she said with a sigh. "You need to cut him some slack. For some people, there is only that one person in life. Annabelle has always been the one for your brother."

Luke shook his head. "Guess he's going to be a bachelor till he dies, then."

"Maybe."

He shot her a look. "Don't pretend that you aren't

hoping his helping her will make them both realize they love each other."

"Don't be ridiculous. Have I ever interfered in your lives?"

"You really want me to answer that?" he said to her retreating back, but she merely laughed.

# Chapter Nine

"What did Annabelle say when she called you?" TJ asked distractedly as she walked with her cell phone to her ear to peek through the curtains at the street below. She'd been writing all day on her latest thriller. That was enough to spook her, a Montana girl living in New York City.

"That's just it," her sister Chloe said with a sigh. "She didn't say anything, really. She just wanted to know why we didn't stay in the house when we were in Whitehorse for Grandma's funeral."

TJ could hear sounds of the newsroom behind Chloe. Like her, she was still at work at the large newspaper where she worked as an investigative reporter. "What did you tell her?"

"That we didn't want to."

"It takes a lot of nerve to call you and demand to know why we stayed at the hotel," TJ said. "She didn't even attend Grandma's funeral. I hope Grandma comes back and haunts her."

"Annabelle did sound scared. I can't imagine staying

in that house. You felt it, too. But I wasn't about to tell Annabelle that was the reason we stayed at the hotel."

TJ shivered and hugged herself with her free arm. "Why didn't you tell her?"

"Tell her what? I'm not sure what I felt—let alone what we might have heard upstairs. I was feeling emotional with grandmother's funeral and remembering going to live there as a girl…and everything."

"We both heard a noise upstairs," TJ said. "It could have been the wind, a branch rubbing against the side of the house or just the house settling. Even though I write this stuff, staying in the house just felt…wrong."

"We are as bad as Annabelle when it comes to sticking our heads in the sand and pretending nothing is wrong," Chloe said. "What if there is something… dangerous going on up there and now Annabelle is in that house?"

"Look, you know Annabelle. She always overreacts to everything. So has she sold the house?"

"She says it will be soon and then she'll be out of there. But you know what it looked like. I would think it would take months just to clean it out, let alone get it ready to sell."

"Chloe, don't you wonder why Grandmother left the house to her and not us?"

"Not really. Annabelle's right. She always was grandmother's favorite. Anyway, if Frannie had left it to all three of us, we would have killed each other over it. The three of us have never gotten along."

"We did once. After high school our lives just kind of went in all different directions. But we're still sisters and Christmas is coming." Chloe said nothing. "I'm glad Frannie left the house to Annabelle."

Her sister chuckled. "I was, too, once that I saw what a mess it was. I like to think it was Grandma teaching her a lesson." TJ laughed. "Can you imagine Annabelle's face when she saw the place?"

Chloe laughed, too, but TJ could hear the hurt in her voice. "The house isn't worth much, so what does it matter?" she asked, letting the curtain drop back into place. It had mattered enough that they'd gotten in a huge fight with their sister and hadn't really spoken for months.

"I suppose you're right."

"I was thinking about going to Whitehorse for Christmas," Chloe said, as if it had just come to her. "Surprise Annabelle. She should have the house ready to sell by then, but if she didn't, maybe help her?"

"Seriously?" TJ glanced outside again, then moved away from the window.

"Remember Christmas in Montana? I wonder if they still have that Christmas dance at the old gym."

"You're really thinking about going?" TJ asked.

"You have to come, too. It's been so long since we've been together. Christmas is the perfect time to patch things up between the three of us."

"I don't know. I have a book out then. My publisher wants me to do a book tour." But TJ was balking at the idea and now that Chloe mentioned it, she was definitely considering Christmas in Montana. Not for the reasons Chloe would have liked, though. "I'll think about it. I have to go." She took another look out the window as she disconnected.

Just the thought of whatever they'd heard upstairs in their grandmother's house—footsteps, the creaking of floorboards, what sounded like their grandmother's walker... The memory made her shudder and she let the curtain drop back again. Frannie's ghost? she thought with a laugh.

Unfortunately there were worse things than ghosts, she thought, as she checked her apartment door to make sure all the locks were engaged.

ONE LOOK AT Annabelle and Dawson could see she'd been crying. He hated that her tears could still affect him the way they did. How had he not seen how hurt and alone she was?

Annabelle leaned against the doorjamb, eyes narrowing. "If you came to get your money back..."

His earlier moment of weakness vanished. He reached over and flicked at her shoulder, making her flinch. "Just trying to knock that chip off your shoulder. I told you. I'm not worried about the money."

"I'll pay you back when I sell the house."

"Fine." He wished he hadn't come here, but the sooner she got the house ready to sell, the sooner it would be bought, even if he had to buy it himself, and then she'd be out of here and things could get back to normal.

Annabelle sighed. "What are you doing here?"

He wished he knew. It had seemed so simple when his mother had suggested it. Help get Annie out of town. But being around her messed with more than his mind or his money. "I'm going to help you pack up the house and take what you don't want to the dump—unless you want to argue about that, too?"

"I know you think I'm a charity case that you have to—"

"You never were graceful when it came to taking help from anyone," he interrupted with a sigh. "Just say thank-you and let's leave it at that."

She clamped her jaw shut for a moment. "I'm also not graceful when people pity me."

He let out a bark of a laugh. "You think that's what this is? Sorry, sister, but you are the last person I feel sorry for. You need to get your grandmother's house ready to sell. You want to sell this house and clear out of town? Fine with me. I have some things to take to the dump. I thought I'd take some of yours." He gave her a challenging look. "But if you don't want my help—"

"Thank you."

He felt his expression soften. She looked dead on her feet already this morning—and even more beautiful even after having been crying. There was something vulnerable about her that he'd only seen a few times. Too bad the cameras had never been able to capture it. She would have been even more famous.

"You're welcome," he said quietly, his gaze still on her. It was hard not to touch her. To run his thumb over those full lips. To brush that errant lock of blond hair back from her soft cheek.

At a low rumble of a growl, his gaze was dragged away. He looked past her to where Sadie had entered the house and now stood just inside the kitchen, the hair standing up on the back of the puppy's neck. From where he stood, though, he couldn't see what the growling was about.

He stepped past Annabelle, worried that the dog had gotten into something she wasn't supposed to. As he entered the kitchen, he found Sadie hunkered down, a low snarl in her throat. What he couldn't see was whatever had her scared. She appeared to simply be growling at the wall.

"Your dog is freaking me out," Annabelle said as she came up behind him.

ANNABELLE SHIVERED AT the eerie, spine-tingling noise the dog was making. "What is wrong with her?"

"Good question. Any reason she would be growling at your kitchen wall?"

"Do you believe in ghosts?" she asked Dawson in a hushed voice.

"Ghosts?" He turned to look at her. "Seriously?"

Annabelle shook off the crazy thought, wishing she hadn't brought it up. "Of course not, but there's a wall that shouldn't be there." She explained about what Mary Sue had told her.

"The plans must be wrong."

"That's what I thought, too, but now..." She glanced at his dog. "Your dog seems to think there's something behind that wall."

"Sadie?" The dog jumped in surprise and, whining, ran to him to cower behind his boots.

Annabelle raised a brow. "I feel like your dog right now."

Dawson was staring at the wall. "I've never seen her

act like that before," he said frowning. "Why would your grandmother wall up an alcove?"

"That seems to be the question of the week." She shrugged. "Makes no sense, huh?" She could feel his gaze on her. When she met his eyes, she saw something that made her soften dangerously inside. "I should get to work." Turning, she headed for the third bedroom that was nearly full of her grandmother's collectibles. She grabbed a couple of empty boxes on the way. Behind her, she heard Dawson talking to his pup. It made her smile since he was asking Sadie what was wrong with her as if he expected an answer.

DAWSON LOADED SADIE into his pickup, cracking the windows enough that he could hear her if she needed to get out. It was a crisp, cool November day, the air scented with dried leaves.

It didn't take him long to load all the boxes Annabelle had stacked at the edge of the porch into the back of his pickup. He stretched, thinking of her doing the same. She came out with more boxes full of what could only be considered junk.

"I'll take a load of boxes to the dump, then pick up more boxes," Dawson called up to the porch.

She put down the box and stretched. "Thanks. I was just going to make some coffee. You want a cup before you leave?"

He shook his head. "I won't be long." She nodded. He could feel her watching him as he drove away. What had made him think this would be easy?

By two in the afternoon, Annabelle had loaded all

the empty boxes he'd picked up up on his way back from the dump. He'd helped with the last few and was glad to see his brother Luke arrive with some friends in the ranch flatbed truck.

It didn't take them long to load everything she had packed up. At the dump, he helped discard the contents of the boxes before Luke cut out with his friends. Dawson knew he could have called it a day, as well. There were plenty of boxes for Annabelle to continue packing—if she felt like it. He didn't know about her, but it had been a long, tiring day.

But instead of going home, he drove back to her house, using the empty boxes as an excuse. Along with thoughts of Annabelle, he couldn't get the hidden alcove off his mind. After he'd parked and unloaded the empty boxes in the spot she'd cleared out in the living room, he went back outside.

Annabelle was busy working in one of the upstairs rooms. She'd only given him a tired wave when she'd seen him. He'd seen her surprise. She'd thought he wouldn't be back.

"Let me know when you have those boxes loaded," he'd called up. "I'll bring them down for you."

He wandered into the kitchen, the wall still bothering him. He tried to imagine why anyone would wall up an alcove. Especially Frannie Clementine. It had to have been the owner before her.

Behind him, he heard Annabelle come into the kitchen and pour herself a cup of coffee. She motioned to him. He declined. He had enough trouble sleeping as it was. The last thing he needed was coffee this late in the day.

"Still confused over the wall?" she asked with a chuckle. "I remembered that my grandmother had a hutch there when I was going up. There was definitely an alcove.

"So the plans are right. Why would my grandmother do that?"

He shook his head, but he suspected whatever was in that small space had enough of a smell that his pup was picking up on it. "Aren't you curious at all about what's in there?"

"No and I have no desire to tear into that wall, if that's what's on your mind. I just want to get this house ready to sell."

"There was only one other time that my dog acted like that, now that I think about it," he said, turning to look at her. "We stumbled onto a calf that had been torn apart by wolves."

"There is no dead calf killed by wolves in my wall."

He raised a brow. "There's something in there. Why else close off the alcove?"

"Why is everyone trying to scare me?" She put down her coffee cup. "It's late. We should probably call it a day."

"If I were you, I'd have to know what's in there."

"You aren't me," she snapped. "As you pointed out years ago, we are nothing alike."

His stomach knotted. It was the first time either of them had brought up that part of the past. "So true. You and I have never wanted the same things. And now you just want to get the house sold and get out of town."

"That's right."

"I won't do anything to slow you up." He stepped past her and started toward the front door.

"It's not that I didn't appreciate your help today," she said, following him out. "Thanks for taking boxes to the dump for me and for getting me more boxes."

"No problem."

"I just don't have time to remodel the kitchen," she said.

He nodded, wanting to take her in his arms and tell her that everything was going to be all right. But he didn't think that was the case. Something was wrong at this house. Maybe there wasn't anything behind that wall. He hoped not. But he could see in her expression that she was running scared and had been for a while.

But he was the last person she wanted trying to comfort her.

He tipped the brim of his Stetson and headed for his truck, all the time mentally kicking himself for the emotions that had his heart aching.

ROB WALKED PAST the house as the last pickup pulled away. Out of the corner of his eye, he saw the young woman standing in the doorway. She pulled off the bandanna that had been covering her long blond hair. Her hair fell to below her shoulders as she turned back inside the house. He could hear her phone ringing as he continued on past.

At the corner, he turned and walked back toward

the house. What he'd been able to find out about Francesca Clementine had left him shaken. Maybe it was a coincidence, but the woman had bought the house right after his uncle's Baby Doll had taken off with his loot from the heist.

Now Rob watched the woman inside the house on the phone. From what he could tell, she was alone. He was thinking of circling around to the back of the house when a neighbor came out onto her porch. She squinted in his direction. Small towns. This one was the worst. Everyone seemed to know each other, which meant he stood out like he was wearing a neon sign.

He gave a short nod at the woman and continued walking. He could feel her watching him all the way to the end of the block before the busybody finally went back. It was the same woman who'd seen him last night around the Clementine house. He couldn't let her scare him off again. That his uncle might be right about this one had him excited. He would get into that house, one way or another. But what to do about the granddaughter?

INEZ GILBERT WAS a confirmed busybody. Anyone who didn't like it could just stuff it. At eighty-nine, she had no patience. Not that she'd had much when she was younger. But now she felt as if she didn't have a minute to waste on ignorant fools. And it seemed to her that the number of those people grew in relation to her advancing years.

She prided herself on being more observant than most people. When she was dead and gone, no one would be able to say that she'd let anyone pull the wool over her eyes. She believed that her advanced years had made her a student of the human condition. One look at a person, and she could size him or her up in a minute. She was hardly ever wrong.

That's why, when she'd seen the man walking down the street, looking hard at the Clementine place, she'd known. Something about the way he was walking, something about the way he was looking, something about the way he was dressed. Not to mention, she'd never seen him before last night and doubted he was from these parts.

Picking up the phone, she called the sheriff's office. The dispatcher tried to put her off, then tried to hand her off to one of the deputies.

"I want to speak to the sheriff," Inez said. "Don't make me come down there."

Finally she was put through to Sheriff McCall Crawford. Now there was a sharp woman. McCall had started out as a deputy, but bypassed several men on her way to sheriff. She was respected in the county and had won each election handily. Inez had made sure that everyone at the senior center voted for her. She'd also canvassed the neighborhood to make sure everyone got out and voted for the woman.

"Hi, Inez," McCall said when she came on the line. "I heard there was a problem in your neighborhood." She sounded friendly and not in the least upset that Inez hadn't wanted to talk to anyone but her.

"I saw a man walking past on the other side of the street. He was obviously a stranger, dressed all wrong, and he was staring at the Clementine place in a way that was suspicious."

"Was it possible he was interested in the house because it's for sale?"

Inez appreciated the diplomatic way the sheriff had put the question and smiled. "That stuffy little Mary Sue Linton put a For Sale sign out in the yard, so, yes, I'm aware. But he wasn't looking at the place like he was thinking what it might go for or if he might want to buy it."

"How was he looking at it?" McCall asked.

"Like he was looking for someone. And tonight wasn't the first time I've seen him sneaking around."

McCALL HAD BEEN dealing with Inez Gilbert for years. Most of the department staff found her to be a pain in the neck. But Inez was smarter than they gave her credit for. The elderly woman noticed things, things that often were worth checking out.

"I'll tell you what, Inez. If you see him again, you call me right away. I'll tell the dispatchers to put you right through."

The woman let out a satisfied harrumph. "He's up to no good. Mark my words. I can tell just by looking at people."

"I know." McCall listened to Inez talk about fools for a while and then got off the line. One of the new deputies was passing by. "Martin," she said, motioning him in. "Do me a favor. When you're on duty could you keep an eye on the Clementine place?"

"On Millionaire's Row?"

She smiled, wondering how that area had gotten the name. Apparently a lot of people didn't know what a million would buy. "Let me know if you see anyone loitering around there."

After he left, she decided to call it a day. Her husband was making dinner tonight since it was his day off as a local game warden. Their daughter, Tracey, would have spent the day playing hard since she was on holiday until Monday.

McCall was looking forward to that time after dinner when Tracey was tucked away in bed for the night and she and her husband could just curl up on the couch together.

But as she was leaving, she couldn't help thinking about the man Inez had seen. The county had been quiet for a long while now. There were the usual disturbances that went with any community. But there had been little crime lately. Most of the calls her department got were barking dogs, kids misbehaving, speeding, car wrecks, underage drinking and minor thievery.

It was one of the joys of living here, she thought as she climbed into her patrol car. Her home was in the country, but she made a point of driving the couple of blocks to go down Millionaire's Row. She'd always liked the large houses with their wide porches, though most of them looked as if they could use a little work.

Still, the trees were huge and beautiful when grown out in the spring and summer. In the fall, the yards would be full of fallen leaves. Only a month ago, she'd seen some of the children playing in them and had thought of her own daughter. There was nothing more fun than piles of leaves. But while the leaves were gone now and the trees were stark against the November sky, the branches were so thick and full that they still provided privacy from the street.

She slowed as she neared the Clementine place. A sports car was parked in the driveway. She'd heard that one of Frannie's granddaughters have returned to town to get the house ready to sell. Maybe that's all the stranger was interested in, she thought. As she drove on by, she saw Inez peering out her front window.

McCall gave a flash of her lights and waved. Inez, always on duty, waved back.

ANNABELLE WATCHED DAWSON drive away, reminding herself why they'd broken up all those years ago. She could tell by the set of his jaw and the ramrod stiffness of his back that he was upset with her. Upset because she didn't want him to take a sledgehammer to her kitchen wall? And why? Out of simple curiosity. Like she had time to remodel the kitchen before she sold the house.

She couldn't help being irritated with him. It hadn't been her idea for him to help her clean out the house.

But the moment she had the thought, all her irritation evaporated. The problem between them wasn't her kitchen wall. It was those old feelings mixed with the chemistry that had always arced between them like a live electrical wire. Being so close together most of the day had been hard on both of them.

She felt close to tears as she wandered back into the kitchen and opened the refrigerator. Of course Dawson had come to her rescue. She glanced toward the wall that shouldn't be there.

"What is it you have to hide, Grandma Frannie?" she asked the empty room.

Unfortunately, the refrigerator was almost as empty as the room. She had a few leftovers from her last grocery store trip, but nothing looked good. She closed the door; her stomach rumbled. Glancing at the clock, she saw that the grocery store was open for another twenty minutes.

But she didn't have the energy to drive the few blocks and shop. Turning out the kitchen light, she wandered down to her bedroom and threw herself onto the bed.

Another day or two and the house would be empty. A day or two of cleaning…maybe painting…

She couldn't think about that now. She was too tired. Unfortunately, her mind was still on Dawson. Pulling out her cell phone, she made the call, thankful when his phone went to voicemail.

"I'm sorry. Thank you for your help today. I really appreciated it." She disconnected.

Changing into a flannel nightgown she found in one of the chests of drawers, she crawled into bed. If her model friends could see her now, she thought, loving the feel of the warm flannel. Her last thought, though, was of Dawson as she closed her eyes and dropped off into an exhausted sleep.

Several hours later, she woke with a start. She listened, trying to understand what had awakened her. That's when she heard it. Someone was trying to break into the house.

ROB SWORE AS he saw a light come on at the house next door. That nosey old woman. She'd run him off last night, coming out on the porch with a shotgun, of all things, and yelling at him like he was a stray.

He moved into the shadows where he couldn't be seen. He'd been in town too long. His uncle called him every day, demanding he get into the house, no matter what he had to do.

"You don't understand," he'd tried to tell Bernie. "There's this old woman who lives next door—"

"You can't handle an old woman?" Bernie had demanded. "Am I going to have to come out there myself?"

He'd gotten off the line in the middle of his uncle's tirade. The old man knew nothing about small-town America. Every time he walked around the neighborhood, people stared at him. All day there were people coming and going from the Clementine place. Tonight, he'd told himself, he would get into the house. The problem was that if he had to kill the granddaughter, he feared her body would be found too quickly. It wouldn't leave him much time to search the place, and from what he'd seen looking in the windows, the house was a mess.

But he couldn't keep waiting. Maybe the granddaughter knew about the loot and was looking for it, as well. He couldn't take the chance that she would find it first.

He pried harder at the window and thought he almost had it when a light came on inside the house, making him swear under his breath.

"Move and I'll blow your manhood to kingdom

come," said a weathered old woman's voice behind him at the same time he felt the business end of a shotgun shoved into his back.

He swung around, grabbing the barrel of the shotgun and knocking the old woman off her feet. She opened her mouth, but he was on her before she could scream. Clamping a hand over her mouth, he swept her up from the ground. Taking her and her damned shotgun, he headed through the bare-limbed trees that separated the two properties.

# Chapter Ten

Dawson woke, head aching. With a groan, he rolled over onto this side and came face to face with Sadie. The look the pup gave him was one of disappointment. "Was I that bad last night?" he asked the dog.

Sadie whined and looked away.

He groaned again, feeling even worse. And all over a woman. Not just any woman. Annabelle Clementine.

Last night, after he'd left her house, he'd started to head home. But then he'd seen Jason's pickup parked in front of the Mint. He'd told himself that he could use a drink. Maybe two. Now he couldn't remember how he'd gotten home.

At the sound of someone in his kitchen, he felt his heart leap. Surely he hadn't gone back over to Annabelle's. And what? Had her drive him home? No.

Swinging his legs over the side of his bed, he saw that he was fully clothed. Hmm. He wasn't sure exactly if that was good or bad. Might depend on how he'd gotten home. He'd never been a drinker—let alone driven drunk. Someone must have helped him off with his boots, though. That meant someone had driven him home last night.

Padding to the kitchen, he peered around the door-jamb, not sure who he would find making coffee—just thankful someone was.

"Jason?"

His best friend turned to grimace at him. "You look like hell."

"I feel worse. Was I...?"

"Drunk?" His friend nodded.

"Morose?"

Jason laughed. "Do you mean did you go on and on about Annabelle?"

Dawson grimaced and headed back down the hall toward the bathroom. "Don't you get tired of being a fool?" he demanded of his image in the mirror. The answer was as plain as the look on his face.

"Talking to yourself again?" his brother asked from behind him, making him start.

"Knock much?"

"You left your door open. You look like hell."

"Thanks. I heard that already." He turned off the water after splashing some on his face and drying himself with a towel. "What are you doing here so early?"

"It's after ten."

He winced as he reached into the medicine cabinet, shook two aspirins into his hand and, chewing them, swallowed them dry.

His brother was grinning at him. "You butt dialed me last night from the bar."

His head began to ache even worse.

"It sounded like you were in trouble."

"Other than having the worst hangover ever, I'm fine."

Luke cocked an eyebrow at that. "So, what is going on with you? If you're going back over to haul more boxes to the dump, I'm sorry but I can't help you today."

"Sure you are."

"That why you have such a hangover?" his brother teased. "Things didn't go well with Annabelle?"

He shot his brother a warning look and walked out of the bathroom to the kitchen where Jason handed him a cup of coffee and offered one to Luke, who heartily accepted.

"So how *are* things going with the two of you?" his brother asked as he pulled up a stool at the breakfast counter.

Dawson didn't even bother to look at Luke, let alone answer.

"Don't get him started," Jason said joining them. "Did I hear that your mother volunteered the two of you for the Christmas Stroll and Parade this year?"

Both groaned. "I hate to ask," Dawson said after taking a sip of his coffee.

"You're going as Santa," Jason said to him and then turned to Luke. "And you're going to be one of his elves."

"Of course I am," Luke said with a curse.

All Dawson could think was that by the time the Christmas Stroll and Parade rolled around, Annabelle would be long gone.

THE LAST PERSON Annabelle expected to see was Dawson. He arrived in his pickup, which she saw was full of more empty boxes. He began to unload them on her lawn. She watched, wondering what he thought he was doing, but at the same time thankful to see that many boxes. She'd been up since daylight, unable to sleep, and had made a half dozen trips to the porch with full boxes already this morning.

She hadn't expected to see him again—not after snapping at him yesterday about the stupid alcove wall. Even with the apology she'd left on his phone. It made her all the more suspicious as to why he was helping her.

Her head ached from lack of sleep. The house had been particularly noisy last night. At one point, she'd thought she heard someone breaking in. But when she looked out, she hadn't seen anyone. After that, she'd gotten up a couple of times only to find the wind whipping tree branches against the outside. Still, at one point, she'd stood at the dark window and could have sworn she'd seen a shadow scurry through the trees and away from Inez's house. The man Inez Gilbert had seen peeping in windows?

She had stared for a long time, but didn't see the shadow again. Still, it had kept her up. At one point, she'd even checked the doors and windows to make sure they were all locked.

Dawson brought a bunch of the boxes up onto the porch. He hadn't seen her standing in the doorway and started when he looked up and saw her. He looked as if he'd had a bad night, as well. He gave her a nod as he went back to pick up more of the boxes he'd unloaded from his truck. Jason and a couple of cowboys she didn't know drove up in pickups and got out. They headed for her, stopped at the edge of the porch for introductions then asked what they could do.

Today she wasn't about to argue. "I have some large things that I need taken down from upstairs to the charity shop," she told them. "Bed frames, side tables and some blankets."

They went to work while she finished filling boxes from upstairs. She'd hoped that she and Dawson might find a minute alone to talk, but he kept his head down loading the boxes she'd filled, seeming just to want to get the work done so he could leave.

On one rare occasion late in the day, both Jason and the crew had taken loads away and hadn't returned yet. She found Dawson on a water break next to the house.

"You don't have to bring your own water," she said as she watched him gulp the cold water from a bottle. It reminded her of when they were kids and shared a hose many times over the summer months.

"I'm fine," he said between gulps.

"You don't look fine." The words were out before she could call them back.

"I might have had too much to drink last night."

She couldn't help being shocked. "That's not like you. At least, not the Dawson Rogers I knew."

"PROBABLY WHY IT didn't take all that much to get me into this shape," Dawson said and finally smiled for the first time that day.

"I didn't expect you back here," she said.

He chuckled at that. "Didn't plan on coming back when I left." His gaze met hers. "I didn't get your message until this morning."

"I am sorry."

"You shouldn't be. We were both tired and I was butting in where I had no business."

She glanced toward the house. "I *am* curious about what might be behind that wall." She chuckled. "Probably just dust bunnies. We'd both be disappointed if we knew."

"Probably," he said, although he knew that wasn't the case. Sadie didn't react like that over dust bunnies. "Maybe it's best if we don't know what's back there or why your grandmother sealed off the alcove. It will just be a mystery." Until the next homeowner realized the space was there and broke into it to find…to find what?

At the sound of Jason returning, they both went back to work. They worked all day. Jason had picked up hamburgers from Joe's In-n-Out for lunch. But that had been hours ago. It was getting dark by the time Jason and the cowboys he'd brought called it a day after loading the last of the boxes. Annabelle thanked them for their help and watched them drive off, leaving her alone with Dawson.

"Why don't I run by the store and get something for dinner?" he offered. He'd taken a peek in her refrigerator when she was out of the room. He doubted she ate much, being a model, but he also worried that she might still be short on cash.

She started to argue that it wasn't necessary, but he

waved off her protests and headed for the store before it closed.

It was late. Very few cars were parked in the lot as he went in, not that he was paying much mind. He was bone weary, and he knew it had little to do with the physical exercise he'd had most of the day or even his hangover.

"So you're back from your hunting trip," said a familiar voice behind him.

Amy. With a mental head slap, he remembered telling her that he'd call her when he got back. For a moment he couldn't think of anything to say. They had dated off and on for the past year. If he had to put a name to their relationship, he guessed it would have been called friendship with benefits.

Not that he thought of it that way. In truth, he didn't give it a lot of thought. That was what was nice about what they'd shared. It was…comfortable. He liked her. She liked him.

"Sorry, I'm afraid it slipped my mind," he said honestly as he turned to face her.

She raised an eyebrow. "Slipped your mind?" Divorced, Amy Baker worked at the local hardware store. He saw that she still had on her vest and, like him, had stopped after a long day of work to pick up a few groceries.

Amy studied him as if looking for something in particular. He could pretty much guess. If she'd heard about Annabelle Clementine returning to town, she was no doubt wondering, like a lot of other people, what was going on. Not that he and Amy had ever discussed his

high school girlfriend. But Dawson knew that someone in town would have told her. It was hard to have
a broken heart here without most of the county knowing about it.

"How was your Thanksgiving?" he asked, recalling
that she planned to go to her aunt's up by the Canadian
border and desperately wanting to change the subject.

Her expression made him feel guilty, but that followed quickly by anger at himself. He and Amy had an
understanding. Both of them could date other people.
Even if he was doing something he wasn't supposed to,
he shouldn't have felt guilty.

He groaned inwardly as she said, "Fine," and turned
her back on him to sort through the oranges.

Glancing around, he told himself that he really didn't
want to get into anything here in the grocery store pro-
duce department. Like the post office, this was where
you eventually saw everyone in town. It was also where
rumors got started like wildfires.

"I'll call you later," he said to her back. She nodded
without turning around.

He paid for the chicken wings, bean salad, rolls and
a six-pack of beer he'd picked up for his dinner with
Annabelle, telling himself he had nothing to feel guilty
about.

But by the time he got back to the Clementine place,
he was in a bad mood. Annabelle picked up on it right
away.

"Your dog pee on your pickup seat?" she asked as
he tossed the food he'd bought onto the kitchen table.

He shook his head. He certainly wasn't going to try

to explain it to this woman. He wished he'd just gone home. What had possessed him to suggest getting them something to eat for dinner? He couldn't really leave Annabelle without any food, could he?

"Make yourself at home. I'm going to change," she said and left the room.

*Change?* He blinked. Change into something more comfortable? Had he given her the wrong impression by suggesting dinner? Now he was really wishing he'd followed his instincts and just left.

ANNABELLE WONDERED WHAT had happened at the grocery store. Clearly something, given Dawson's change of mood. She could tell he wished he hadn't suggested getting dinner. She'd smelled the spicy chicken wings the moment he'd walked in the door and heard her stomach rumble.

As she changed out of her dirty clothing, she wished she'd taken a shower while he was gone and changed then. Instead, she'd kept working. Her mind was set on getting this house ready to sell. It occupied all of her thoughts—except when Dawson was around.

"I'm so glad you got chicken wings," she called from the bedroom as she finished changing. No answer, but she didn't let that bother her. She was betting he got bean salad and rolls and beer. That was what he used to get when he planned one of their picnics out in the wilds. The man was a creature of habit. That used to drive her crazy. Now it felt…wonderful and sweet and made her heart ache.

She thought about him coming back this morning,

even though he was clearly hungover. That, too, was like Dawson. He wasn't one to whine. Or to take a day off when there was work to do. That he'd come back at all to help her made her heart beat a little faster. It also made her feel guilty. She'd treated him poorly before she'd left and now he was overlooking that to help her.

To get you out of town as quickly as possible, she reminded herself. He wanted her gone. When an old high school friend called after hearing she was back in town, Annabelle had asked if Dawson had anyone in his life.

"I heard he's been seeing Amy Baker for a while," her friend had told her. "But I get the impression it isn't serious. Why? You aren't falling for him again, are you?"

"No, of course not. I'm just here to sell the house. Dawson and I…well, lightning never strikes in the same place twice, right?"

"Wrong," her friend had said with a laugh. "Is there a storm brewing?"

When Annabelle walked into the kitchen, Dawson looked up in surprise. He blinked, taking in what she was wearing and then seeming to relax. Had he forgotten she was there?

"You changed," he said, looking almost embarrassed.

She frowned. "Is that a problem?" She'd put on the T-shirt and jeans that she'd purchased the other day.

The food he'd brought was spread out on the table. She saw that he'd opened a can of beer and was drinking it as he glanced at the contents of the metal box she'd left on the table. Dawson was going through the photos and yellowed newspaper clippings from inside it.

She sat down across from him.

"Help yourself," he said of the food. He stopped looking at the contents of the metal box to enjoy some of the food he'd brought, the two of them eating in companionable silence.

"So what do you make of these?" he asked after a while, as he slid his beer toward her and motioned to the box.

She took a drink before she said, "I haven't really looked at anything in it. I found it under the floorboards in my bedroom. When I opened it, I didn't recognize anyone. Must be from before Frannie moved in."

Dawson shot her a look before he pushed one of the photos in her direction. "Check this out." He went back to reading the newspaper clipping next to his paper plate.

She glanced at the old black-and-white photo. It appeared to be four people in some kind of nightclub setting. Two women, two men. All were dressed to the nines. Other than that, she couldn't imagine what he'd found of interest.

As she pushed the photo back toward him, she saw that he was frowning. He put the newspaper clipping down and looked at her.

"What?" she asked.

"Did you see it?" he asked and nodded toward the photo he'd given her.

"Apparently not." She was tired and the beer was making her lethargic. She would much rather just sit here with him than look through old photographs of people she didn't know.

"Look hard at her," he said, putting his finger under the face of the prettiest of the two women.

She picked up the photo. The woman's pale hair was long and fell over one shoulder. Her figure was quite voluptuous for a woman who was small in stature.

Then she looked into the woman's light eyes and felt her heart begin to pound. "Frannie?"

Dawson chuckled. "Frannie was quite the looker in her younger days, wouldn't you say?"

"That can't be her. This woman is blonde."

"Blonde like her granddaughter."

"But Frannie always had red hair."

He lifted a brow. "Well, at one time, she was a blonde."

Annabelle stared at the photo. It was her grandmother. She hadn't recognized Frannie because she'd looked so different from the grandmother Annabelle had known. And she didn't just look different, she was dressed differently. Frannie had never worn makeup in all the years Annabelle had known her. But in the black-and-white photo, she was clearly wearing dark lipstick and mascara and eyeshadow.

It was a shock seeing Frannie so young—and sexy—and blonde. The young woman in the photo was smiling broadly and standing next to a handsome man in a pin-striped suit. Annabelle couldn't help but smile back at her grandmother. Frannie looked so happy. Was this the man Frannie had said was her alleged husband? Annabelle had been shocked to find out that Frannie had never married. So who was the mysterious man who'd fathered her son? Could this man be Annabelle's grandfather?

Annabelle speculated that Frannie's white lie about a husband who never existed might have been one reason they hadn't met her until their parents were killed and their grandmother insisted they come to Whitehorse to live with her.

"Even more interesting is the man with her." Dawson carefully smoothed out the old newspaper clipping. It was yellowed and cracked. "His name according to this is Bernard 'Bernie the Hawk' McDougal. He was an Irish mobster."

"What?" Annabelle quickly skimmed the newspaper clipping before staring at the man's mug shot. "He was arrested for a famous heist?"

"Arrested and released for lack of evidence," Dawson said. "The jewels were never found."

She picked up the photograph of her grandmother again.

"Wanna bet they were lovers?" he said. "Check out the way the man is looking at your grandmother."

"You're reading a lot into a photo." Even as she said it, though, she knew he was right. She couldn't help but think of a photo of her and Dawson that she'd kept all these years from their senior prom. The way Dawson was looking at her in the shot—the way she was looking at him… She knew what love looked like.

Her gaze rose to meet his and she wondered if he remembered the photograph. Or if he'd kept his copy. A lump formed in her throat, but it was nothing like the knot in her chest.

"Your grandmother was a gangster's moll," he said with a laugh. "Who would ever have suspected it?" He was grinning at her as he reached for the beer they'd been sharing—just as they had when they were lovers all those years ago. Their hands brushed. She started to pull away, but he caught her, entwining his warm fingers with her own. His grin disappeared. His eyes darkened and his breath seemed to catch.

Her own breath began to come quicker as she lost herself in the warmth of his gaze. She felt her lips part. His gaze shifted to her mouth. Her heart pounded so loudly she couldn't hear anything else. He was going to kiss her.

He gave a slight tug on her hand as he leaned toward her. She held her breath, remembering Dawson's kisses and yearning for this older, even sexier version of him to kiss her as he had on the dance floor that night at the bar.

He was a breath away. She closed her eyes as she closed the last of the distance. Her lips brushed over his, just a feather touch. She leaned in farther.

Her eyes came open abruptly as he let go of her hand. She blinked. He'd pulled away and was now shoving back his chair and rising.

"I've got to go," he said, his voice hoarse with emotion.

"Dawson." She'd wanted that kiss, needed it, and yet as she got to her feet, she knew kissing him again was the stupidest thing she could do. Hadn't Jason warned her not to lead his friend on? That was definitely not what she'd meant to do. As soon as this house sold, she was out of here.

So why did she feel like crying?

BACK AT THE RANCH, Dawson mentally kicked himself as he built a fire and fed Sadie. The pup quickly fell asleep in front of the crackling blaze while he paced, still angry with himself.

He should have been tired after all the boxes he'd loaded and unloaded today. But he felt antsy. At the sound of a vehicle pulling up out front, he moved to the window to see Amy park and get out. He swore under his breath as he opened the door before she could knock.

"I got tired of waiting by the phone," she said, as she stopped at the foot of the porch steps.

"I'm sorry. I've been…busy."

"I heard." She glanced past him into the house. "Is she here now?"

It wasn't like he had to ask whom she was referring to. "No. She's never been here."

Amy nodded and came up the steps. "I thought we should talk." She didn't give him a chance to tell her that he was tired and wasn't in the mood. Clearly she didn't care.

As he followed her inside, he realized that she felt he owed her an explanation. It surprised him, since what they had wasn't serious. At least, for him.

As she turned and he saw the tears in her eyes, he felt a start. It was his night for surprises. Clearly Amy had seen their so-called relationship a lot differently than he had. He thought of his mother's warning.

"Don't hurt that girl," his mother said when he and Amy had first started up after years of random dating.

"She knows it isn't serious," he'd said, and his mother had rolled her eyes.

"It's been serious for her since the first time you took her to your bed."

"It was her bed," he'd said, making his mother roll her eyes again. "Stop trying to get me married off."

"That's not what I'm doing. You shouldn't marry Amy. You should marry someone you can't live without."

"Is this reverse psychology?" he'd joked, uncomfortable with the conversation because there'd only been one woman who fit that bill. And while he and his mother could talk about anything, this was one topic he'd prefer not to discuss with her.

Now, as he looked at Amy, he knew that Willie had been right, as always. He'd thought he and Amy both knew that this wasn't going anywhere. "Amy, I'm sorry I didn't call you."

"This isn't about you not calling me when you returned from your hunting trip," she said. "Although you did say you would."

He nodded. "You're right. Something came up."

Amy let out a bitter laugh. "Something? Don't you mean *someone*?"

"Look, it isn't what you think."

She scoffed. "You didn't just say that."

He groaned inwardly, thinking the same thing.

"It's her, your high school sweetheart, the one who broke your heart."

Yep, he thought, that was the county grapevine's short version of him and Annabelle apparently.

"Annabelle—"

"I know her name," Amy snapped. "Annabelle Clementine. A supermodel no less. What I didn't know was that if she ever came back you would drop everything to be with her."

"That might be the way it looks, but…"

"I don't want to talk about her," Amy said with a shake of her head. She looked around the room for a moment. He could see that she was barely able to hold back the tears.

"I think I know what you want to hear," he said. Her watery gaze met his. "You know I like you." One tear broke loose and cascaded down her cheek. "I enjoy being with you."

"But you don't love me." She nodded. More tears followed.

"I thought that's how you felt about me, as well."

"You never suspected that I might want more?"

"I didn't have more to give," he said, hating himself. His mother had tried to warn him. He should have seen this coming. But he hadn't thought about the future. He'd been living day to day since Annabelle left. "I never wanted to hurt you."

"So you're back with her."

"Good God, no," he said, surprised that she would think that.

She made a swipe at the tears. "Then what is going on?"

"I'm helping her clean out her grandmother's house so she can get it sold and leave town."

Amy stared at him. "You really believe that."

"It's the truth."

She laughed and shook her head again. "And then what?"

"And then nothing."

"You're going to let her leave again?"

"*Let* Annabelle leave?" It was his turn to laugh. "You don't *let* a woman like Annabelle do anything. She's like a force of nature. She does whatever she wants, when she wants, and the best thing you can do is get out of her way before she mows you down."

Surprise registered on Amy's expression. "You make it sound as if you don't even like her."

He took a deep breath, held it for a moment as he considered what she'd said. As he let it out, he said, "Sometimes I want to strangle her. Other times…"

"You're still in love with her."

He started to deny it, but she cut him off.

"All these years? You never got over her. Were you just waiting for her to come back?"

"No." He shook his head adamantly. "I never thought she would come back. Why would I wait for her? Only a fool would…" He swore under his breath. "Like I said, it isn't what you think."

She lifted a brow, clearly not believing a word of it. "She's the one, the one you will always be in love with. The one that got away, the one you will compare all other women to and find them lacking. Is it possible you didn't realize that before she came back? Seriously?"

He felt as if he'd been blindsided. "Look, you have it all wrong."

She was shaking her head. "Stop lying to yourself

and worse, to me. We're friends, right?" He nodded, glad she wasn't crying anymore. "So do something about this. If you love her, then don't let her leave again. Tell her."

He laughed and took a step back. "I did that thirteen years ago."

"If you don't, then you aren't the man I thought you were." With that, she turned and walked out, leaving him standing in his living room wondering why she couldn't understand how wrong she was.

"Annabelle doesn't love me. She never did love me. At least, not enough," he said as the door closed behind Amy. He listened to her pickup drive away before cussing Annabelle for coming back and messing up his life yet another time.

# Chapter Eleven

Annabelle spread everything from the metal box out on the kitchen table after Dawson left. Once she'd recognized her grandmother in the one photo, she'd been able to find her in others. Bernie, the mobster, was in his share, as well, along with his "associates."

Her grandmother used to tell these outrageous stories of when she was young. She and her sisters had never believed a word of them.

But, it appeared, there'd been some truth to them—maybe more than Annabelle wanted to acknowledge. As she glanced through the contents of the metal box, she reminded herself where she'd found it. Was it coincidence that her grandmother had hidden it under the floorboard in the bedroom Annabelle had stayed in for years growing up? Did her grandmother assume Annabelle would choose to stay in that room when she came back to sell the house?

If the floorboard had been loose and something hidden under it from the time she was a girl until she left at eighteen, she would have noticed it. She was sure of that. Which meant her grandmother had left it for her—just as she'd left her the house. So there was a message in here.

But, for the life of her, she didn't know what it was. Frannie's name was never in the newspaper cutlines. Under one photo, she was referred to as Baby Doll. What was that about? Maybe the woman just looked like here grandmother.

Then why would Frannie have the photos and newspaper clippings?

As she read the news articles, it left little doubt that her grandmother had been involved in some dangerous business as the moll of mobster Bernie McDougal. These men that her grandmother had partied with were criminals. Could it be possible she hadn't known at the time?

Doubtful, Annabelle thought. Her grandmother had been a sharp woman. Annabelle suspected Frannie had known exactly what she was dealing with. She thought of the grandmother she'd known—a soft-spoken, ladylike and diminutive woman. Now, though, she realized there was a lot more to Frannie than anyone in Whitehorse had suspected.

In the clippings, she'd also discovered something that gave her a chill. The heist that Bernie McDougal and one of his associates had been hauled in for questioning about had never been solved—nor the rare jewels ever recovered. But what sent shivers up her spine was that it had been less than a year later that Frannie had bought this house in Whitehorse.

Annabelle recalled her grandmother saying that she used the money from her deceased husband's insurance policy to buy the house. Frannie had been pregnant and given birth not long after that to Annabelle's father, Walter Clementine, said to have been named after the father he'd never known.

Now Annabelle knew that the husband had been a lie. So who was the father of her baby? Carefully she put everything back into the metal box. She couldn't shake the feeling, as she glanced at the wall hiding the former alcove, that she'd only found one of her grandmother's secrets.

That her grandmother had known these men… It made her shudder. Worse, her grandmother had left this for her. Why? Was she trying to warn her?

At the sound of someone on her porch, she jumped. A moment later the doorbell rang. She stuck the metal box into one of the kitchen cupboards as the doorbell rang again. She felt jumpy, almost afraid to see who was standing on her doorstep.

Peering out through the red-and-white gingham curtains, she saw Mary Sue. The Realtor spotted her about the same time. Annabelle quickly dropped the curtain and opened the door.

"Is everything all right?" Mary Sue asked suspiciously.

"It's fine."

"You just had such a weird expression," the woman persisted.

"You startled me, that's all. So, do you have a half dozen prospective buyers to tell me about? How about one?"

Mary Sue shook her head. "I came by to see how

you were faring. I heard Dawson and his friends have been helping you."

"No secrets in this town," Annabelle said under her breath as she stepped out of the way to let the Realtor see how much had been accomplished. "All but one of the bedrooms is empty. One bathroom is done and the other one getting there."

"You still have a lot of things to get rid of," Mary Sue noted as she took in the items piled up in the living room.

"These are all to be either sold or donated. I called the antique shop. Mary said she would come look to see if there is anything she can use. I wanted to wait until I had a chance to go through the kitchen."

"You are making progress, I'll give you that," the Realtor said, then *tsked* at the state of the walls in the emptied bedrooms. "Those are going to have to be painted."

Annabelle sighed. "Did you just come by to torment me?"

Mary Sue seemed surprised. "Is that what you think I'm doing?"

Annabelle didn't answer for a moment. "I'm just tired and out of sorts." Mary Sue would be, too, if she'd been working day and night to empty out this place. She hated to imagine how the Realtor would be if she'd just learned that her grandmother had left her a houseful of junk—and box full of disturbing secrets.

"So, you and Dawson…"

Annabelle gave her an impatient look. "Really? Have you had any interest in the house?"

Mary Sue shook her head. "It's a bad time of the year with Christmas coming."

Annabelle groaned. Before she could escort the Realtor out, she had to listen to Mary Sue's other suggestions regarding paint color, possible new appliances, even the replacing of all the carpet in the house with hardwood.

She let out a sigh of relief when she was able to close the door behind Mary Sue. That's when she noticed the dark car parked across the street and realized it wasn't the first time she'd seen it there.

It was, however, the first time she'd realized there was a figure sitting at the wheel behind the tinted glass.

DAWSON OFTEN WENT for a horseback ride to clear his head. Unfortunately, it hadn't done much good today. He kept thinking about his mother's earlier visit and what she'd said about Annabelle. As if Annabelle wasn't on his mind enough.

But he had made a decision, one he thought even his mother would support, he thought as he returned from his ride.

"We got Annabelle's house pretty much cleared out, but you're right, she needs more help." The words were barely out of Dawson's mouth before his mother took off her apron, tossed it down and said, "So, what are we doing standing around here? Let's pack up some food. I'll get your brother up to help and make a few calls."

When he hesitated, she asked, "That is what you want, right? Jason told me how hard you all have been working to help her get the house ready to sell so she can leave."

He nodded. "That's the plan, remember?"

Within minutes, his mother was on the phone lining up able-bodied men and a couple more trucks.

"I already helped," Luke said when he was rousted from bed.

"So I heard. But today we're getting everything out of the house to begin cleaning and painting," she said, making her youngest son groan. "Get a few of your friends to meet us at the Clementine place."

Luke groaned. "If I call them this early, they'll kill me."

"Tell them your mama said if they don't get up and meet us there—"

"Got it." He threw back his covers, then quickly pulled them over himself again. "Could I have a little privacy?"

"Like you have anything to hide," Dawson joked from the doorway.

He had no idea what kind of reception they were going to get once they reached Annabelle's grandmother's house, but he didn't have to worry.

The moment they drove up, Annabelle opened the door, looking both leery and surprised. She'd already filled a dozen more boxes and had them sitting at the end of the porch.

His mother was out of the truck in a shot, her arms full of food as she charged toward the door.

"Willie?" Annabelle said and looked to Dawson for clarification. As if he could control his mother once she set her mind to something.

"Point me to the kitchen." But his mother was already headed there by the time Dawson reached the edge of the porch.

"I'm going to need your keys to move your car," he said to Annabelle.

She looked a little dumbstruck as two more pickups arrived, both full of boxes. Luke trudged toward the house, a carton full of cleaning supplies in his arms.

As if sleepwalking, she reached back inside for her keys. When she dropped them into his palm, he gave her a quick nod.

But before he could turn away, he saw surprise and something more in her big blue eyes. Gratitude? Surely nothing more. That night outside the bar after he'd kissed her, she'd told him to stay out of her business. Then, last night, she'd seemed willing when he'd kissed her, before his senses had come back to him.

She couldn't be anymore confused than he was about last night. But, in his defense, she'd been real clear about him leaving her alone and he hadn't been listening. Still wasn't. But that didn't mean she hadn't been sincere in what she wanted—and didn't want—from him.

"Dawson," she began.

"Annabelle?" It was his mother calling. She seemed about to say something more to him, but turned back into the house as Willie asked where they should begin. Luke's friends simultaneously began to bring in the cardboard boxes.

Dawson didn't see much of Annabelle after that. He kept busy hauling the last loads to the dump. Willie had put Luke's friends to work filling boxes with old newspapers and magazines and dragging them out to the porch. If anyone could organize an army, it was his mother.

They broke for lunch. By then, Willie had managed to get both spare bedrooms and a bathroom cleaned. She put Luke and his friends to work painting.

"Neutrals," Willie said in response to Annabelle's surprise. "I called Mary Sue and asked her what we should paint the rooms. I just happened to have some paint. I hope you don't mind."

But Dawson could tell that she didn't believe his mother had never-opened gallons of neutral colors just sitting around anymore than he did.

"I can't tell you how grateful I am for all of this," Annabelle said, her voice breaking. "I don't know how to thank you."

Willie reached across the table to squeeze her hand. "No need. We're practically family." She shot Dawson a look that said they would have been family if it wasn't for him.

He lowered his head and sighed inwardly. His mother didn't think he'd done enough to try to stop Annabelle from leaving thirteen years ago. Maybe she was right about that. But ultimately, nothing on this earth could have kept Annie in Whitehorse—certainly not him.

ANNABELLE COULDN'T MISS the look that passed between mother and son. Dawson appeared uncomfortable, taking a sandwich from the plate his mother passed around and going out to the tiny back porch rather than eating it in the crowded kitchen.

"I'm sure this is your doing," Annabelle said when

she joined him on the porch with a sandwich of her own. She sat down beside him to let her legs dangle over the side, much as she had when they were kids.

"My mother?" He shook his head. "You know how she is. She likes to help."

"And she just happened to have a lot of neutral-colored paint she wanted to get rid of."

He grinned over at her. "I told her how anxious you were to get the house sold…" He shrugged.

She looked off into the distance to the line of trees that marked the edge of the Milk River. The backyard was still lush in places, even after a hot summer and long fall. But she could tell the temperature was dropping. Soon the cold and snow would set in. She had to be out of here by then.

"How are you holding up?" he asked.

She smiled, knowing what she must look like in her grandmother's hand-me-down clothes, her hair under a bandanna, smelling of dust and old musty things. "I can see the floor now in all but a couple of the rooms. I'm feeling…better."

He nodded. "What about your grandmother, the photos, the newspaper clippings?"

Annabelle shook her head. "I still can't believe it. Frannie used to tell us stories about these outrageous parties she went to when she was, like, seventeen and all the crazy things men would buy her, furs and diamonds…" She laughed. "We never believed a word of it. I mean, look how she lived here in Whitehorse. I can assure you, there are no furs or diamonds that I've run across in this house."

"I would agree if I hadn't seen the photos."

She drew out the hem of the dirty sweatshirt she had on. "Most everything I've found in her closet looks like this, only with gaudier designs. Frannie didn't even own a car and she used what was left in her bank account to pay the utilities and taxes so I'd have time to sell this place." Her voice broke. "This house was all she had when she died."

She could feel the heat of his gaze as he looked over at her. "She had more than this house. Everyone in town loved her. She was always doing for others. She was rich in friends. To her, that was more important than furs and diamonds," he said as he finished his sandwich and got to his feet.

"You mean her values were better than mine."

He stopped and looked at her. "I wasn't comparing the two of you." He brushed again at the invisible chip on her shoulder.

"Last night…"

"I shouldn't have kissed you," he said quickly and looked away. "You've made it clear how you feel about me, this town, Montana in general."

Had she? "I'm not even sure how I feel about a lot of things," she said, looking up at him.

Willie called from the doorway. "I thought I would start cleaning the kitchen cabinets unless there is something else you'd rather I do."

"No, that's great," she said, pushing to her feet as Dawson hopped off the porch to walk around front. "I'll come help you."

DAWSON OFTEN FOUND himself in awe of his mother. Just watching her in action was a sight to see. The afternoon passed in a blur of activity. The house smelled like cleaning products and paint, which was much better than dust and decay.

"We paint the kitchen tomorrow and finish the rest of the rooms," Willie was saying. "I expect all of you back here after work tomorrow to help."

Luke's friends nodded. His mother commanded respect. He knew no cowboy stupid enough to go against Willie.

Annabelle started to object but his mother cut her off saying, "I'll bring my chocolate cake." As if anyone needed more incentive.

That got grins out of Luke's friends. Willie's chocolate cake was famous.

Dawson hadn't said two words to Annabelle since their talk on the back porch. Mary from the local antique shop had come up and taken what she wanted. After everything had been removed from the house except for a chair in the living room, the bed and dresser in Annabelle's old room, and the kitchen table and chairs, they called it a day.

Everyone began to leave. His mother packed up a few things to take home. When Dawson offered to carry them out to his pickup—since the two of them had ridden in together—his mother waved off his help. "I'm riding with Luke. See if there is anything else you can help Annabelle with."

As if he was fooled by that. Annabelle wasn't, either.

"Thank you, but you've done more than enough," she said as Willie left.

She and Dawson eyed each other in the silence that filled the house following his mother's exit.

"Look, I know you said—"

"Thank you." She met his gaze. "It would have taken me weeks to accomplish all of this…" Her voice broke.

He shrugged. "You needed help. That's what people do here for neighbors." Then he tipped his hat and left, headed straight for the bar. "See you tomorrow," he said over his shoulder.

# Chapter Twelve

"What are you doing?"

At that moment, Annabelle was wondering why Mary Sue was calling her, let alone asking her such an inane question. There was music playing in the background and the sound of drunken voices.

"A few people from high school thought you might want to come down to the bar for a drink." She sounded as if those few people were holding a gun on her, forcing her to make this call. A few people from high school? "We're down at the Mint. If you're interested…" Mary Sue also sounded like she'd already had a drink or two. "You have something better to do?"

Now, that really was the question, wasn't it? "I just need to shower and change."

"Great. See you soon." Mary Sue disconnected.

Annabelle considered calling her back and declining. What had she been thinking, saying she would go? But really, did she have something better to do? Fall into bed exhausted. That also had its appeal, but she headed for the shower. When was the last time she'd been out with a bunch of women? She thought of her clubbing days and groaned inwardly. Those days were gone and she wasn't even sure she missed them.

Showered and changed, she pulled her hair up and drove down to the Mint. A glass of wine sounded perfect. Maybe two. Then back home to bed.

The moment she walked in, she spotted Mary Sue with a handful of young women she wasn't sure she recognized. But as she approached the table and each of the women greeted her, she began to remember them. Mary Sue had traveled in a different circle than Annabelle had in high school. But the school had been small enough that she'd still known everyone.

Mary Sue got her a glass of wine and some of the others pulled up a chair for her. There was the usual chatter around the table—men, mothers and work. Fortunately none of it was about her or why she was back in town. She figured Mary Sue had warned them not to try to interrogate her. She was just starting to relax when she saw Dawson nursing a beer alone at the end of the bar.

DAWSON LOOKED UP from his beer and saw her in the mirror over the bar. He swore under his breath. What was Annabelle doing here? Had she followed him?

He turned on his bar stool, surprised to see that she'd showered and changed, unlike him. She was sitting with a bunch of women, women she'd never associated with in high school. But they all seemed to be getting along as if old friends. Go figure.

He turned back to his beer, determined that she wasn't going to ruin it for him.

At the sound of a commotion and sudden raised voices, he turned, shocked to see that Annabelle was at the center of it. A bar patron who'd clearly had too much to drink was trying to pull Annabelle to her feet, demanding a dance.

"You think you're too good for us since you became some hoity-toity cover girl?" the man demanded in a loud, drunken voice. "You too good to dance with someone like me?"

Annabelle was trying quietly to tell the man that she was just there visiting with friends and didn't want to dance. "I appreciate you asking, but I'm really tired."

"Tired?" The man scoffed and jerked her to her feet and into his arms.

Dawson swore, put down his beer, slid off his bar stool and strode up behind the man. He recognized him as a cowhand from up north by the name of Clyde Brown. He laid a hand on the man's shoulder. "Let's leave the lady alone," he said.

"Lady?" Clyde scoffed as he looped his arm around Annabelle's waist and started to haul her toward the dance floor.

"Let her go," Dawson said quietly, afraid he could see how this was going to play out. Definitely wasn't what he'd had in mind when he'd come here for one beer and a little peace, if not quiet.

"Stay out of this if you know what's good for you, Rogers," Clyde snarled drunkenly.

And just as he'd figured, the cowhand shoved Annabelle. She crashed into the table edge, drinks going everywhere, as Clyde spun around, leading with his fist.

Dawson saw it coming long before the cowhand took the swing. He blocked it and grabbed the cowhand by the back of the collar. "I don't want to fight you. So let's just—"

"She ain't worth fightin' over?"

Dawson looked past the man at Annabelle. Before he could answer, Clyde broke free and took another swing.

From behind Dawson, he heard the cowhand's friends get up from where they'd been at the bar. He swore under his breath as he coldcocked Clyde and swung around to take on the rest.

## Chapter Thirteen

Her face flaming from humiliation, Annabelle drove back toward her grandmother's house. She would never think of it as hers. It was her grandmother's, and she was suddenly angry that Frannie had left it to her. True, she needed the money from it to save herself, but right now she could overlook that.

In fact, the more she thought about it, the more she was convinced that Frannie had collected all that junk, filling the house full, just to keep her granddaughter in town for as long as possible. Not that that theory made any sense.

Within a block, she realized that the last place she wanted to be right now was in that house. She turned at the next street and headed east out of town. She had no idea where she was going. A part of her realized she was wasting precious gas, but at that moment, she didn't care.

The night was dark. There was no one on the highway. She drove mindlessly, wishing she never had to stop. The fact that she had nowhere to go after she sold the house terrified her. She had no plan, wouldn't have much money and had no idea what to do next.

At a sign for Nelson Reservoir, she turned off and drove down to the lake. The water shimmered even in the blackness of the dark night. She got out and walked to the edge of the shore, thinking about throwing herself into the icy-cold water. The thought actually made her laugh. As bad as things were, she still wanted to live.

She thought of Dawson, probably still back at the bar fighting those men—and all because of her. She kept seeing the expression on his face when the man he called Clyde had asked if she was worth fighting over.

Annabelle shook away that image, still embarrassed. Dawson had fought the man for her. He'd come to her rescue. Again. She shook her head and breathed in the night air. Mary Sue had gotten her out of there as the bar had erupted into a half-dozen fistfights. She'd passed a patrol SUV, lights and sirens blaring, headed for the bar as she'd left.

If only someone would make an offer on the house. Now it was more than a desperate need for the money. She had to get out of this town. She had to get away from Dawson before she ruined his life as well as her own. Right now he could be sitting in a jail cell because of her. If so, she didn't even have the money to get him out. She owed him money for keeping her car from being repossessed, as it was.

She groaned, suddenly chilled by the November air, and headed back to her car. Just the thought of Dawson choked her up. Why did he have to be so nice to her?

She'd hurt him. Why couldn't he act like a jackass and make her glad that she'd left him as well as Whitehorse?

On the drive back, she reminded herself that the house was coming along nicely—thanks to Dawson and his family. Tomorrow most of the rooms would be finished, then there was no reason Mary Sue couldn't start showing the house. By this time next week…

As she pulled into the drive, her headlights flashed across the front of the house. Her breath caught in her throat. She slammed on the brakes, her eyes widening in alarm at the sight of someone inside the house. She cut the lights and sat in the dark staring, telling herself that as upset as she was, she had to have imagined—

The figure moved past the window.

Annabelle threw the sports car into Reverse and stepped on the gas. The car roared backward and into the street. At the sound of screeching brakes, headlights filled the inside of her car. She had only an instant to realize how close she'd come to being hit before her car door was jerked open.

"WHAT THE HELL?" Dawson demanded as he reached in and pulled her keys. "Are you drunk?"

Annabelle stumbled out from behind the wheel and into his arms. He could feel her trembling. "There's someone in the house."

"You can't just back up like that without looking," he snapped before her words registered.

She turned her face up to him. It looked ghastly white. Even her bow-shaped mouth was trembling. "In the house. I saw someone."

Her actions began to make sense as he looked from her to the house. "Stay here."

She nodded, those blue eyes wider than he'd ever seen them.

He considered moving the cars out of the middle of the street, but figured if she really had seen someone in the house... He still had her keys in his hand. "A house key on here?"

She pointed to a large square one.

"Get back in your car out of the cold and stay there."

"Maybe you should call the police."

"I just had a long talk with the sheriff, so no thanks."

"Then be careful."

Was she actually worried about him? He'd fought four cowboys because of her and held his own pretty well. While her concern was touching, he knew it was just something a person said when they were sending someone into a house after an intruder.

As quietly as he could, he crossed the porch to the front door. He listened for a moment before slipping the key into the lock. Slowly he turned the knob.

The door swung open. A now familiar fresh-paint smell rushed out at him. He listened, heard nothing while he waited for his eyes to adjust to the semidarkness before he stepped in and turned on a light.

He figured if there really had been someone in the house, they were long gone by now. They would have heard the commotion out in the street. They would have seen Annabelle's headlights when she pulled in.

But he wasn't taking any chances as he moved quietly through the house, checking one room after another. There was no sign of anyone. He checked the back door, still locked—just as the front door had been. He checked windows, all locked.

He walked through the living room into the kitchen and turned on the overhead light. Again, no sign that anyone had been here.

He went to the wall concealing the alcove, recalling Sadie's reaction. He'd just squatted down to inspect the white beadboard wainscoting when he heard a sound behind him.

Shooting to his feet, he spun around only to find Annabelle standing in the doorway. She still looked terrified. Her gaze met his. He shook his head, telling himself he shouldn't be surprised that she hadn't done what he told her to—stay in the car.

"Is he gone?" she asked and saw Dawson's expression.

"I couldn't find any sign of anyone being here. Everything is locked up tight. Nothing looks disturbed, not that there is much to disturb at this point."

"But I saw…" She swallowed and shook her head. "Someone." She met his gaze, hoping he would tell her it was possible. She could see that his knuckles were skinned and there was a cut on his cheek near his right eye, the skin around it bruised.

"The place was locked up tighter than a drum. If someone broke in… I didn't see it."

She hugged herself. "So, you're saying I imagined it."

He wasn't saying anything. He looked down at his boots then finally lifted his gaze to her. He saw her bristle. "It isn't that I don't believe you thought you saw something…

"Why are you here?" she demanded.

He felt himself balk at her sudden anger. Right now, he had no idea. "I thought that after what happened at the bar… I only wanted to check to make sure you were all right. I'll move your car."

She said something he didn't catch as he started past her and caught a hint of her perfume. It had the same effect on him that it had thirteen years ago. He increased his stride as he headed for the front door. Remembering how she felt in his arms only minutes ago in the middle of the street, he feared that if he even hesitated, it would only make him do or say something foolish.

"I'll bring you back your keys," he said as he walked out the open front door, thankful his senses were starting to clear in the fresh air of the porch. But as he turned, he saw that the keys he'd left in the door were gone and Annabelle had pulled her car into the drive, but his pickup still sat in the middle of the street. Something about that seemed to mock his behavior tonight.

Hearing her behind him, he said over his shoulder, "Lock up behind me." He almost added that if she had any more trouble tonight to call him. "Call the sheriff if you see anyone around the house again."

He was almost to his truck when he heard the front door of the house slam as if caught by the wind. He looked back to see her pass by the front window. All he caught was a glimpse of her, since she'd turned out all but one of the hall lights. But he could tell that she was crying.

The sight stirred his earlier protectiveness. "Damn it, Annie," he said under his breath. "Why do you have to keep doing this?"

The night had no answer. He saw a light come on in her old bedroom and felt an ache that threatened to double him over.

He had to get her out of Whitehorse. Get her house sold. Get her on the road. No matter what it took. Otherwise… She was going to get into his heart again.

And yet, even as he thought it, he feared it was too late.

ANNABELLE KNEW WHAT she'd seen. A man moving through the house. No ghost of her grandmother, even though, for a moment, there had seemed to be a white light around the figure. No doubt a reflection from her headlights. She didn't believe in ghosts.

She moved through the house searching every closet and cubbyhole, checking the windows and doors herself, turning on all the lights. Dawson was right. The house was empty. All the windows and doors had been locked.

He hadn't believed her. Worse, when she'd come into the house, she'd found him inspecting that stupid wall in the kitchen. Did he think the intruder had escaped through it, somehow?

Exasperated, tired, upset and generally irritable, she stood in the living room trying to decide if she was going to leave all the lights in the house on tonight. It seemed silly, but she was tempted. Angry with herself for being such a chicken, especially given that apparently she'd only imaged the intruder, she went through the house turning off lights until she reached her bedroom.

She was still annoyed with Dawson and realized she had no good reason to be. He'd worked here at the house all day, he'd saved her at the bar, he'd driven over to check on her, he'd braved coming into the house to look for the intruder…

The man just couldn't stop saving her. He must be getting sick of it. Hadn't he pretty much told her that the only reason he was helping her with the house was to get rid of her more quickly?

Well, it wouldn't be quick enough for either of them, she told herself as she started into her bedroom on the first floor and froze.

The loose floorboard where she'd discovered the metal box with Frannie's photos and newspaper clippings was sticking up just enough that only she would notice it. Her heart began to pound as she looked around the room. The board wasn't the only thing out of place.

Her pulse a steady panicked throb in her throat, she saw that someone had moved her bed.

## Chapter Fourteen

Annabelle stood nailed to the spot, her mind racing as fast as her heart. *Someone had been in the house.* Dawson wouldn't have pried up the floorboard, but he might have moved her bed when he was searching before she came in.

The thought sent a chill through her, because when she'd searched the house minutes ago, she hadn't looked under the bed. She glanced toward the closet. All that was in it were her grandmother's ugly clothes. No trespasser.

Edging toward the bed, she stopped next to the disturbed floorboard. With her toe, she pushed it back down, knowing whoever had been in here hadn't escaped that way. Now that she was closer, she could see where the legs of her bed had scraped across the floor all the way to the wall. How strange. The bed had definitely been moved.

Slowly, she bent down to peer underneath.

At first, all she saw were dust bunnies, relieved not to find a man hunkered under there. But then she saw something that sent her already thundering heart into overdrive. A scrap of fabric was caught in the corner of one of the floorboards. *Another secret hiding place, Grandma Frannie?*

Rising, she went to the side of the bed. It was heavy, the headboard and footboard made of solid wood. But she got it to move an inch at a time until the bed finally stopped at the wall.

The scrap of fabric appeared to be a gray and white stripe. She touched the cloth. Not an ounce of dust on it. Nor were there any dust bunnies on a large portion of the floor.

As she moved closer, she saw a spot on the floor that had been carved out like…like a handhold. Blinking, she realized what she was seeing. A trapdoor.

She started to try to lift it, but quickly thought better of that. What if the man she'd seen was down there? She pulled out her phone. Her first thought was to call the sheriff. Her second was to call Dawson.

Annabelle was so tired of needing to be saved that she pocketed her phone and went into the kitchen to her grandmother's utility drawer. Willie had managed to get all the top cabinets and some of the lower ones cleared out and cleaned earlier today, but they'd decided to leave this drawer for now because it held all kinds of keys, screws, bolts, nuts and tools, all things that they might need before they were finished.

She brought out the hammer and hefted it, gauging its weight, then grabbed a small flashlight that she quickly found worked. Hurrying back into the bedroom, she found the trapdoor was just as she'd left it. If the in-

truder was down there, he hadn't tried to get away, because the scrap of fabric was still caught in the corner.

Leaning down, she grabbed the handhold and lifted.
The door was heavy but she managed without having
to put down the hammer. It groaned upward. She saw
that a table leg had been attached so the door could be
propped open.

Cautiously she shone the flashlight beam into the
gaping hole, surprised to find several wooden steps that
dropped down into blackness. What was down there?
The piece of cloth that had been caught in the door flut-
tered down into that darkness. She aimed the flashlight
beam into the space, only to see what appeared to be
a passageway.

Annabelle listened, chilled to her soul at the sight.
*Oh, Grandma, what were you involved in?* She thought
of Dawson earlier on the back porch painting Frannie as
a saint. Did saints have hidden trapdoors under beds?
Or secret passageways dug under their houses?

There was no way she was going down there. Not tonight. Maybe not ever. Exhaustion pulled at her. Slowly
she closed the trapdoor. In the kitchen, she dug some
nails out of the utility drawer. Back in the bedroom,
she pounded four nails through the door and into the
floorboards next to it. A crude job, at best, but effec-
tive. She put the hammer aside and pushed her bed
back into place.

If someone was down there, he wasn't getting out. Not
tonight. She told herself she would deal with it tomorrow.

# Chapter Fifteen

Annabelle had been hoping to get Dawson alone to tell him about the trapdoor. It was proof that she hadn't been mistaken last night or overreacted or been trying to get his attention. Or whatever it was that he'd thought.

He arrived again with his mother and brother and a small crew armed with rollers and paintbrushes. Everyone fell into line with Willie cracking the whip. Drop cloths were put down, paint cans were popped open, rollers and brushes were handed out and in no time the once-dingy walls took on new life.

Annabelle and Willie emptied the rest of the cabinets in the kitchen and cleaned them in preparation for the painters. Dawson had hauled away the last of the junk. All that was left behind was what Annabelle would need to live here until the house sold.

Willie had asked if Annabelle wanted her to empty the closet in her bedroom of her grandmother's things, but she'd declined, saying she would do it later. The truth was, the clothes were the last of her grandmother's belongings. She'd kept the cookie jar where Frannie had put her "loose change" as well as a few other personal things including several boxes of Christmas tree ornaments, but the truth was, her grandmother hadn't had much worth hanging on to.

"Tell me," Willie said as they cleaned the last cupboards. "What was it like, modeling?" She sounded genuinely interested.

Annabelle rinsed out the rag she'd been using before she answered. "It was hard work. Hardly anyone believes that. They think you just stand there, turn one way then another, smile and go about your day. It was hours of shooting, often either in the cold or the heat. And that wasn't even the worst part."

She stopped, realizing that she'd said more than she'd originally planned. But Willie was looking at her expectantly, as if waiting for the rest.

"There is the not eating, but you get used to that. The working out every day of the week to keep in shape. The always being made up in expectation of someone snapping your photo on their cell phone and selling it to the tabloids, with an accompanying story about how sick you look, how fat, how tired, how ill-dressed. So you're always 'on' except when you're alone in your apartment."

"I'm guessing that still wasn't the worst part," Willie said.

Annabelle let out a bitter laugh. "No. There are the men who have power over your career and the desperate young faces who want your job. At first, it was wonderful, unbelievable. The parties, the money, the famous people you get to meet, seeing your photo on the cover of a magazine." She shook her head. "But none of it is real. Your photos are all doctored. That's not really you on the cover or in the ads. Because even if you look good, you don't look good enough without Photoshop."

She took a breath, shocked that she'd let all of that out—especially to Dawson's mother.

"So, you're going back after you sell the house?" Willie asked.

Tears stung her eyes. "I don't have a choice. I'll never work again at the level I did before, but it's all I know."

Willie scoffed at that. "We all have choices. Some are harder than others. What I'm hearing is that you feel trapped. Sounds like you're the only one who can change that. Just make sure you don't latch on to the first life raft that comes along. It wouldn't be fair to anyone to find yourself trapped in some other way, now would it?"

Just then, Luke came in to announce that the other rooms were done.

But Annabelle had gotten the message loud and clear. *Willie's son wasn't a consolation prize for the mistake she'd made with her life.*

After a quick lunch, Annabelle and Willie painted trim in the bathrooms, neither talking. Willie'd had her say. Annabelle didn't blame her for the warning.

Several of the crew had to leave, which left Dawson and Luke to paint the kitchen.

"I can't believe how different this house looks," Willie said after they'd cleaned their brushes and wandered through the finished rooms. She stopped at Annabelle's bedroom. "You sure we can't paint this room today? We can move the bed and—"

"I'd like to do this one myself," Annabelle said.

"Sure, sweetie, if that's what you want."

"I appreciate everything you've done," Annabelle said quickly.

Willie patted her arm. "Honey, we were glad to help. Now you can get it on the market."

She nodded, afraid she would cry. There was so much she wanted to say. She'd hurt this woman's son, and yet here was Willie helping her. Or maybe she wanted Annabelle out of town so she didn't hurt her son again.

WHEN THEY WERE finishing up for the day, all Dawson wanted to do was make a quick getaway. But his mother seemed to be dragging her feet. The house was coming along nicely. The only room that hadn't gotten painted was Annabelle's bedroom. According to his mother, she wanted to paint that one herself.

More than likely she was just ready for them all to clear out. He knew *he* was ready. Every moment he was around her, he was intensely aware of her. It wore him out. It was time to let them both get on with their lives.

He'd just picked up the cooler his mother had packed and started for the door, when Annabelle said, "Dawson, could I speak to you for a moment?"

He knew he must have looked like a deer caught in headlights.

"Privately?" She motioned him back into the house.

"I'll catch a ride with Luke again," his mother said quickly and grabbed up her belongings. "I need to talk to him anyway." She was out the door before Dawson could argue.

Now, with just the two of them alone in the house, he shot Annabelle a weary look as he put down the cooler. "If this is about last night…"

"There's something I need to show you," she said without preamble and headed for her bedroom.

He watched her go for a moment before following. At the bedroom door, he stopped. She was standing by the bed. For a moment, he thought she'd brought him in her to…to do what? Seduce him?

She shoved the bed with all her strength, sending it skidding across the floor until it hit the wall.

He blinked in shock, his mind racing. What the—

She pointed at the floor. His mind was still on Annabelle standing next to a bed in her bedroom and him thinking… His gaze dropped to the floor. He stared.

"Are those nails?" he asked. They were sixteen-penny nails, large enough that even with half of them embedded in the wood, the other half was sticking out a good three inches. All he could think was that she'd lost her mind—until he saw the handhold carved into the floor and realized he was looking at a trapdoor.

"What the hell?" he said as he moved closer.

She nodded at his surprise.

"Did you know that was under your bed?"

"Not until last night when I came back into my room and found my bed had been moved."

So they were back to her believing that someone was in her house last night?

"Remember the metal box I told you I found under the floorboards? That same floorboard had been pried up and hadn't been pushed back down all the way. I knew someone had been in here. When I knelt down, I saw that the dust bunnies under the bed had been disturbed. Also there were marks on the floor where the bed had been moved."

He had to give her credit, that was pretty observant of her. When he'd searched her house for an intruder, he hadn't noticed any of that. "It must just be an opening to the crawl space under the house. Did you—"

"I took a look, but no, I didn't go down there. But *someone* did. I found a piece of cloth caught on the trapdoor. It hadn't been there long since there was no dust on it."

He stared at the trapdoor with the nails sticking out of it for a moment. "I'm assuming you have a hammer."

She reached over to the bureau, retrieved the hammer and handed it to him. "That's not all. Remember the metal box with the photos and newspaper clippings? I had put it in an empty drawer in the kitchen. Well, it's gone."

He looked up at her. "But it didn't appear that anyone had broken into the house. Unless…" He glanced down at the trapdoor. "Sorry, I didn't believe you last night."

She nodded, seeming to let it go.

It took a few minutes to remove the nails. She'd hammered them down pretty good. He handed them to Annabelle, and after the last one, she gave him a flashlight. It was small and not all that powerful, but he figured he wouldn't be going far. He'd seen trapdoors in other homes that were merely a way to get down to the crawl space if needed.

That's why he was surprised when he shone the

flashlight beam down into the hole and saw the footprints on what appeared to be steps. He glanced at Annabelle. She flashed him an impatient look that said maybe it was high time he started trusting her. Now that was definitely something he wasn't going to ponder right now.

"I'll go down and see—"

"I'm going with you." She had her arms crossed, and her jaw set, and determination burned in those blue eyes.

"I can tell you right now there are going to be spiders, cobwebs, maybe even mice and only God knows what else down there."

ANNABELLE DID HER best to hide her shudder. "I'm going."

He shook his head. "Suit yourself, but don't say I didn't warn you."

She still had the bandanna covering her hair and wore the baggy jeans and ugly sweatshirt. Perfect for a tour of the hidden space under the house.

Dawson took a tentative step onto the top stair, then dropped down the next three. The steps were wide apart. When he reached the earthen floor, he turned to offer her a hand. She hesitated only a moment before taking it. Even with his help, she had too much momentum and ended up in his arms.

He chuckled. "If that's all you wanted, we could have stayed up in your bedroom."

"Funny," she said, pushing herself off his rock-solid chest.

He turned to shine the flashlight beam under the house. "Huh?"

She too was surprised to see that they were standing in what appeared to be a narrow trench. "Isn't this awfully deep for a crawl space since we don't have to crawl?" she asked.

He shot her a look. As he shone the light toward the rear of the house—and the darkness, he said, "If you are still determined to come along, stay right behind me."

Once away from the trapdoor, the damp, earthy air became close. The flashlight beam punched a small hole into the absolute blackness ahead. She grabbed hold of his tooled leather belt. When she tried to see around his broad shoulders, a spiderweb hit her in the face. She shuddered and wiped crazily at it with her free hand.

"You all right back there?" he asked, amusement in his tone.

"Fine."

He stopped. The flashlight beam flickered upward and she saw that they had reached the back of the house. "Watch your head," he said as he ducked under the edge of the foundation.

This time when she glanced past him she saw that this underground space didn't end under the house. It made a sharp right-hand turn and then appeared to keep going. They would have to either crouch down or crawl.

"What is this?" she whispered, although she doubted anyone could hear them this far underground. That thought sent a chill through her.

"It appears to be a tunnel."

"A tunnel? A tunnel to where?"

"Good question," he said. "I'm not sure you should go any farther. We have no idea how long it's been here. If it were to cave in—" She started to argue, but he stopped her. "One of us needs to be able to call for help if the other doesn't come back. You want to see where it goes? Or…" He turned her around. "Or do you want to make your way back to the bedroom? Just keep walking until you reach the light." As much as she hated to admit it, he made a good point. "Give me five minutes once you reach the bedroom. If I'm not back, call for help because part of your backyard would have caved in on me."

"Maybe you shouldn't—"

"Sure you can find your way back?"

She swallowed the lump in her throat and nodded. He gave her a little push and she started walking. It was pitch black all around her. She put out her hands. Spiderwebs brushed her fingers. She stumbled and had to grab hold of the dirt bank next to her. She thought she heard a scampering sound and wanted to run.

But she kept her gaze on the faint light ahead and walked as swiftly as possible. When she reached the steps up into her bedroom, she turned to look back. All she could see was darkness. Not even a faint flashlight beam.

She pulled herself up the steps into her bedroom, grabbed her cell phone and set the timer for five minutes. That's when she saw the spider on her sweatshirt sleeve.

Annabelle had been a runway model, but she'd never undressed that fast in her life. Opening the window, she tossed the clothes and bandanna, spider and all, out the window. She could still feel spiderwebs in her hair.

Phone in hand, she streaked across the hall to the bathroom. Turning on the shower, she jumped in, letting the warm water wash away the dirt and dust and spiderwebs as quickly as possible. The alarm would be going off in a few minutes. If Dawson hadn't come back…

DAWSON FOLLOWED THE TUNNEL, aware of the fresh prints in the soil ahead of him. Annabelle was right. Someone had recently been in this tunnel, which would explain how someone had gotten into the house without breaking in.

As he shone the flashlight into the blackness ahead, his mind raced. How long had this tunnel been here? Had the first owners of the house dug it? For what?

He'd read stories about secret passageways. In Mexico, wealthy Spanish silver families years ago had tunnels dug under their houses to get their families and silver out in case of an attack by outlaws. But what would a family in Whitehorse have to fear? What would a sweet old lady like Frannie Clementine have to fear? Or to hide?

He thought of the newspaper clippings and the walled-up alcove. *Oh, Frannie, what secrets did you have?* Maybe more to the point, why leave the house just to Annabelle? *Was there something here that you wanted only her to find?*

His flashlight beam shone on what appeared to be more stairs ahead. Reaching the end of the tunnel, he climbed up a step to push on another trapdoor. It creaked open, but only a fraction of an inch. That was enough though to see where the tunnel ended—in the old garage behind the house. Someone had pushed several heavy bags of sand onto the door. To hide it?

WHEN THE ALARM on her phone went off, Annabelle was just stepping from the shower and ready to call the sheriff for help if Dawson hadn't— She let out a shriek as the bathroom door swung open and jumped back into the shower to cover herself with the plastic curtain.

"You do realize that shower curtain is see-through, don't you?" Dawson drawled as he stepped into the steamy room and turned off her phone's alarm.

"You scared me half to death," she snapped. "I was ready to call the sheriff so we could start digging for you. You could have knocked."

"I did. When I saw your clothes flung all over the yard, I got worried."

"There was a spider…"

He nodded, still looking at her. She had to give him credit, though, his gaze was on her eyes. But she could tell that he was enjoying himself. He'd caught her at a distinct disadvantage.

"Well?" she demanded.

"The tunnel kept going all the way to the old garage. There was another trapdoor. Someone had pulled several bags of sand over on it recently, I would suspect so no one else found it."

"I wasn't asking about that. I meant that you should leave the bathroom and let me get dressed."

He glanced around. "It seems you didn't remember to bring anything to wear. It's a good thing the tunnel didn't cave in on me."

"I was ready to call for help." She cocked her head at him. "A gentleman would leave."

He chuckled at that, his gaze locking with hers. "You and I are way past that, Annie."

Her heart did a dip-tee-doo at the sound of the pet name. He'd only called her that when they were alone and always when they were intimate. The heat of the shower had warmed her cheeks, but nothing like the sound of that cherished name on his lips.

Without breaking eye contact, he handed her a towel.

Her pulse throbbed under her skin as desire rippled through her. In his eyes, she could see that he remembered what they'd shared right down to the last kiss, the last caress, the last time they'd made love.

She let go of the shower curtain to pull the towel around her. When she did, his eyes definitely weren't on hers.

# Chapter Sixteen

Rob walked along the edge of the Milk River. He could only assume it had gotten its name because it resembled chocolate milk. The river was more like a wide ditch. It backed up onto Frannie Clementine's property.

After the old lady had been a problem, he'd known he couldn't keep walking around the neighborhood. Unfortunately, there were a lot of old ladies like her. Driving past was almost as bad. He swore most of the neighbors spent their time at the window looking for trouble.

He'd gone through the metal box of photos and newspaper clippings last night. If he'd had any doubt that Francesca Clementine was his uncle's Baby Doll, he no longer did. He had to get back into that house, but it had been a beehive of activity. He'd watched box loads of belongings being hauled out.

After following one of the trucks, he'd realized with a sinking feeling that all of it was going to the dump. All but some old furniture that he'd seen dropped off at a local charity shop. What if the granddaughter didn't realize what she was throwing away?

He told himself that wasn't possible. She wouldn't

throw away priceless gems. He had to believe what he was looking for was still in the house.

Anxious, he wanted to end this. The motel in town was adequate but nothing like his home in New York. The weather was colder and he couldn't get any of the food he'd grown accustomed to in the city. It made him jumpy and irritable. Everywhere he went he saw cowboys and pickups. Last night he swore he heard mooing cows. He'd looked out his window to see a semi parked across the street. Sure enough, the back was loaded with cattle.

"I have to get out of here," he said to the wintry-looking landscape. The temperature had dropped and a fog had rolled in. Now everything was covered with frost. He kept slipping on the icy grass along the edge of the river. So help him, if he fell in, he was going to kill someone today.

Last night he'd seen the trapdoor in the old barely standing garage and thought he'd hit the jackpot. But once he'd dropped down in it, he realized it was a tunnel. Following it, he'd ended up in one of the bedrooms. It had taken all of his strength to move the bed aside enough that he could get the trapdoor all the way open.

Once inside, the house had proved to be uninteresting. He'd found the metal box with the photos and newspaper clippings, confirming what he already knew. Francesca had been Baby Doll. But that's all he found.

So what was the point of the tunnel? He hadn't had enough time to search the house well. He didn't think the loot was hidden in the tunnel. It seemed more like an escape route. The old lady must have had it installed in case someone discovered who she was, what she'd done and just how much stolen loot she had gotten away with.

Now he stopped at the back of the house. He could see only a portion of it through the dense, bare-limbed trees and the rock wall next to the river. On the other side was the old garage. He studied the property for a few long minutes trying to decide what to do next. From what he'd seen in the house, the crew who'd been helping the granddaughter should be about done.

The granddaughter would finally be alone. He was counting on it. The first step would be seeing what she knew. Then disposing of her. He could hide her body in the tunnel while he tore the house apart.

He'd been so sure that the woman in the obit wasn't his uncle's Baby Doll. Then he'd been certain that, if she was, she'd blown the loot long ago. Then he'd discovered the tunnel and that had changed everything. The way he saw it, Frannie Clementine had the tunnel dug as an escape route in case she was found out. She would have been afraid of what Bernie would do if he found her. The woman wasn't stupid.

But if she was that afraid, then Rob's instincts told him she probably lived on the cash and gold but wouldn't have dared fence the jewels. She would have known that Bernie and his associates were all waiting for even one of the pieces to surface. Which meant the gems were still in that house. All he had to do was find them.

"YOU KNOW WHAT this means," Dawson said, rising up on one elbow.

She looked into his eyes, her heart pounding. When she'd awakened, all she could think was that this was what everyone had tried to warn her about. But being with Dawson had felt so right. She still loved him. Had never stopped loving him.

That didn't mean she knew what she wanted to do with the rest of her life. She thought about Willie's warning.

"You know what we have to do now," he said.

A dozen thoughts raced through her mind. Her mouth went dry. Did he think because they'd made love and fallen asleep in each other's arms that it meant she was back? That they would take up where they'd left off? All her conflicted feelings for him aside, her life was a mess. She couldn't commit to a paint color if she had to, let alone what she wanted to do with the rest of her life right now.

"We have to bust open that wall in the kitchen."

She stared at him in disbelief. "What?" That was the last thing she'd expected him to say. He must have seen her relief because his brown eyes dimmed a little. His look said, *It's okay, Annie. I know you don't want me.*

Annabelle wanted to cry out that it wasn't true. She'd never wanted anyone the way she did him. But everything was so complicated right now. She would never know if he'd just been an easy way out. Worse, he'd never know if that hadn't been the case.

DAWSON HAD SEEN the panic on her face when they'd awakened in each other's arms. The passion was still there between them, the chemistry, even the love. Last night had proved it. But it wasn't enough to keep her in Montana, maybe especially with a Montana cowboy like him. She'd been out in the world. She'd lived a glamorous life. Being a ranchwoman was a far cry from the way she'd been living in California.

"Annie, the tunnel, the metal box, all of it," he said, hoping she didn't see his disappointment. Had he really expected last night to change anything? "Who knows what other secrets your grandmother had, but given what we do know…we have to open that wall."

A laugh escaped her. He saw her relief and felt his heart drop even more. Obviously last night hadn't meant the same things to her that it had to him. Still, he wouldn't have changed anything. They'd wanted each other, needed each other. Even as he'd taken her in his arms, he'd known it was temporary and he hadn't cared one damn bit.

This morning…well, only a fool would have thought that making love with her would change everything.

"WE HAVE TO look at all the evidence," Dawson said as he climbed out of bed and began pulling on his clothes. So they weren't going to talk about last night. Apparently they were back to business as usual, which meant getting this house sold and her gone.

"No woman has an escape tunnel unless she has something to hide," he was saying.

She felt bereft as she watched him dress and leave her bed. As much as she wanted to call him back, to try to explain… "Maybe the original owner—"

"The original owner didn't have it dug. This was the

bedroom you grew up in, right? Was that escape hatch under the bed?"

She shook her head. Nor had the board been pulled up to hide a metal box. But there had been an alcove in the kitchen that was now gone. She didn't want to believe that any of this was true because of what it said about her grandmother. What it said about Annabelle herself. There was a reason her grandmother had left only her the house, she was starting to realize.

"We're talking about Frannie," she said as she got up and quickly dressed. She saw that Dawson had retrieved her clothing from the yard, sans spider. She dropped it into the hamper and put on her own jeans and one of her new T-shirts. "You remember Frannie? Local do-gooder, tiny, sweet, always helping others."

"I remember her. But you're forgetting. Sweet Frannie had a past. She was a mobster's moll."

She turned her back to him as she dressed. "We don't know that," she argued over her shoulder. "Just because she had her photo taken with that mobster a few times…" She knew she was clutching at straws, but this was Frannie. The grandmother she wanted to believe had left her the house because they were so much alike.

Slowly she turned to look at Dawson. He was so handsome that sometimes it took her breath away. Big, strong, broad shouldered, slim hipped and all cowboy. But also tender and sweet and as trustworthy as the day was long. "You're determined to tear into that wall, aren't you?"

"Just as determined as you are not to touch it. I know you're scared…"

He had no idea. She swallowed. She'd come this far. "Okay."

"We have to open that wall," Dawson said. "We have to know what's back there. Maybe nothing."

"You don't believe that."

"No, I don't. All these secrets… You have to admit, walling up the alcove like that…"

She nodded.

"I promise to fix it better than new so you can sell the house. I'll do it quickly so it doesn't hold up the sale. If there is nothing behind it, you'll be gaining an alcove. It will add to the value of the house."

Annabelle mugged a face at him. "And if there is something behind that wall that shouldn't be?"

He shrugged. "Better to find out now than later."

She headed into the kitchen, suddenly scared. She hoped her grandmother had merely lost her marbles, decided she didn't like the alcove and had someone come in and wall it up. Or maybe she did the work herself. Her grandmother was a master at a lot of things around the house, as Annabelle recalled.

Now that she'd remembered the hutch that had been in the alcove…that meant that her grandmother had to have closed up the space sometime in the thirteen years that Annabelle had been gone.

"I have a sledgehammer in my toolbox in the back of the truck," Dawson said from behind her. "And a better flashlight."

Annabelle nodded and listened as he hurried out to his pickup. Her gaze was on the wall. In the morning light, it appeared innocent enough. It was what might be behind there that had her terrified. *Oh, Grandma, how many secrets do you have?* Maybe more important, what was Frannie expecting her to do about them?

Dawson returned quickly. He hesitated, looking over at her. She nodded and he hefted the sledgehammer.

"You want to do the honors?" he asked.

She shook her head. She didn't want to know what was behind there. She'd already learned enough disturbing things about Frannie and feared they were about to learn even more.

Dawson stepped back and swung the sledgehammer, making a huge hole in the Sheetrock. He swung again, making an even bigger hole. The third time, the Sheetrock crumbled enough that they could see into the hole.

He put down the sledgehammer and picked up the large flashlight he'd brought from his pickup. This one had a broad, strong light. Glancing at her, he said, "Ready?"

She nodded. There was no going back now. She stepped to the hole as Dawson shone the light into the darkness beyond it. The first thing that hit her was the smell.

He let out a curse. Annabelle couldn't speak. *Oh, Frannie, what have you done?*

# Chapter Seventeen

Sheriff McCall Crawford stepped into the kitchen. She'd never been in Frannie Clementine's house. Few people had. While always up for helping others, she'd kept to herself the rest of the time. McCall had known the woman was a hoarder and her house was full to the brim. No wonder she didn't have friends over—not even her neighbor Inez Gilbert.

"In here," Dawson Rogers said now, as he motioned toward the large hole in the wall at the end of the room. McCall wondered if he and Annabelle Clementine were back together since her return. News of the supermodel's return had the entire county talking— and speculating.

He handed her a flashlight. McCall took it as she looked at Annabelle standing with her back to the kitchen counter, arms crossed around her, a scared, stony, shocked and worried look in her eyes.

Turning on the flashlight, McCall stepped to the hole and shone the light in. What she saw shouldn't have surprised her. When Dawson had called and said they'd found something at Frannie Clementine's house that they thought she should see, she hadn't been sure what to expect. Being in law enforcement she was seldom surprised.

At first, all she could see was the rotted, once-clear plastic the body had been wrapped in. Sometime over the years, the decaying body stuffed in the hole had burst the rotting plastic. It appeared that the gelatinous remains of the body had run out, soaking into the floorboards. The rest of the body had rotted along with the plastic and was now little more than a gluttenous blob and bones.

With a sigh, McCall straightened and looked at the granddaughter. "You have any idea who this might have been?" she asked.

Annabelle shook her head. Her blue eyes were wide with shock and fear and no doubt revulsion.

McCall looked to Dawson. "How about you?"

"Not a clue."

"Any reason you decided to look in this wall?" the sheriff asked and listened as he explained about his puppy's reaction. "So this used to be an alcove that you believe your grandmother walled up?"

"For obvious reasons," Dawson said before Annabelle could answer. As he did, he reached over and took the young woman's hand, making McCall wonder again what their relationship now was. Idle curiosity, since everyone in the county knew that she'd broken his heart when she left town all those years ago.

This latest discovery would only add to the intrigue, McCall thought as she looked past them to the window.

A small crowd had gathered. Taking a quick inventory, she realized someone was missing.

"Has anyone see Inez lately?" she asked.

ANNABELLE LOOKED AS if she was in shock. "You can't stay here tonight," Dawson said, feeling guilty. He'd been determined to open up this wall even though he'd known she hadn't wanted to. Had he expected to find a body? Or was he thinking he might find the missing jewels from the Marco Polo exhibit heist they'd read about in the newspaper clippings Frannie had saved in the now missing metal box?

"I have a guest room," he added, seeing how anxious Annie already was.

"He's right," McCall said. "You can't stay here. In fact, I need you both to clear out while we take care of this." She turned to the deputy who came through the door. "Run over to the neighbor to the south and see if Inez is all right."

The deputy seemed surprised that Inez wasn't already over there finding out what was going on. Clearly so was the sheriff.

She looked to the two of them. Annabelle seemed rooted to the floor. "If you need to get a few personal things," the sheriff said, "do that. I'll let you know when you can get back into the house."

Dawson already had Annie's hand in his. Hers was freezing cold. He gave her a little shake. "The sheriff needs us out of here."

"Who is that?" she asked, motioning toward the former alcove.

"We won't know for a while," McCall said and looked to Dawson. "You'll see that she's okay?"

Those words finally seemed to bring Annabelle out of her stupor. She nodded, saying, "I'm fine," even though it was clear she wasn't. She numbly followed him out to his pickup. The street was full of people. Some called to him, asking what was going on. He merely shook his head and hurriedly loaded Annabelle into the passenger seat, then ran around to slide behind the wheel.

Annie was staring at all the gawking people. "Everyone is going to know what Frannie did."

He wanted to argue that they didn't know it had been Frannie's doing, but he doubted she would believe that any more than he did. Once they'd seen the photos of her with the mobster, they'd stopped being sure what Frannie might have done.

He drove toward his ranch. Annabelle stared out the side window, appearing to fight tears. "I'm sorry," he said.

"It's not your fault."

"I never should have opened that wall."

She finally looked over at him, her blue eyes swimming. "She had to have killed him and then closed off the alcove to hide his body." She shook her head as if trying to chase away the memory of what she'd seen. "This is why she left me the house and not my sisters."

He wasn't sure how that computed.

"I just don't know what I'm supposed to do with this," she said. "She wanted me to know about her past.

She left it all for me, including what we found behind the wall."

"I doubt your grandmother meant for you to find the body," he argued.

She gave him a patient look. "Why do I feel as if all of this is a warning?"

NEWS OF THE discovery traveled like quicksilver through the town. Rob heard people talking about it everywhere he went. He wasn't sure what rumors to believe. But the bottom line was that a body had been found in the house—and no jewels, as far as he knew.

Back in his motel room, he called his uncle and told him.

"They have any idea who the man is?" Bernie asked.

What shocked Rob was that his uncle didn't sound all that surprised. "Not yet. Why? Do you think you know him?"

Silence, then finally Bernie said, "I might."

Rob swore. "Someone you had looking for her?"

"I had a lot of people looking for her. Mickey Frazer, remember him?"

"Wait. He disappeared like fifteen years ago?"

"Maybe less than that."

"I thought the speculation was that he got hit by the Italians."

His uncle chuckled. "I might have started that rumor since he was always fighting with a few of them."

Rob couldn't believe this. "So how did he end up dead in some wall in Whitehorse, Montana?"

"If I had to guess? He found Baby Doll and she did

him in, stuffed him into a wall and covered up the whole thing before he could contact me with her location. If that was his plan. So, what about the jewels?"

"The place is now crawling with cops," Rob complained. He wasn't about to tell his uncle that part of the reason was the death of the neighbor, a woman named Inez Gilbert. She'd been found at the bottom of her basement stairs with a broken neck. "If any of the loot is left—"

"It's there and I want it, understand?"

Oh, Rob understood perfectly. "How do you expect me to find it—if it is there? They are still digging Mickey's remains out of that wall. If the gems were in there with him... Well, they're gone, okay?"

"She wouldn't have put them in the wall with a guy like Mickey Frazer. No, she would have hidden them somewhere else. Remember, the woman was smart, cagey. So find the jewels."

"I don't get it," Rob said. "Why take the jewels if she wasn't to sell them or fence them?"

"Truthfully, I think she thought she was saving me from a prison sentence. As it turned out, she probably was. The Feds turned the city upside down looking for those gems. They would have found them if Baby Doll hadn't absconded with them. Maybe she thought she was doing me a favor."

"Yeah, I bet that was it."

"Just find them."

Rob stared at his phone, realizing that his uncle had hung up on him. He cursed a blue streak as he disconnected. A thought struck him. Once the cops were through over at the house, he could get into it. The granddaughter wouldn't stay there now. He knew how to get in—and out—without notice. All he had to do was wait until the cops cleared out.

"WE GET AN ID on the body?" County Attorney Rand Bateman asked from McCall's doorway.

"Frannie made it easy. The man's leather wallet was in the hole with him." She picked up the plastic bag with the New York driver's license in it and held it up. "Michael James Frazer. From what I've been able to find out, he was involved in the Irish mob in New York City."

"Cause of death?"

"The coroner found blade marks on his ribs."

Rand shook his head. "Unbelievable."

"That's not the half of it." She motioned to her open computer. "Ever heard of the Marco Polo Heist?" He shook his head. "Me, either. Way before my time. But fifty-six years ago, it was big news. Several men died during the robbery. Only one was believed to have gotten away, Bernard 'Bernie the Hawk' McDougal, an Irish mob kingpin. The men killed all worked for him. There was never enough proof to arrest Bernie, but he was questioned about the heist, according to what I've found out so far."

"What could any of that have to do with Frannie Clementine?"

McCall leaned back in her chair. "Michael 'Mickey' Frazer would be seventy years old now if he had lived. But that's not the interesting part. Guess who he worked for?" She nodded. "Bernard McDougal. Although Bernie was suspected in the Marco Polo Heist, he was never convicted and the gems were never recovered. Now one of his men ends up dead walled up in Frannie's house. The coroner says he's been there for from ten to fifteen years."

Rand swore under his breath. "So the body wasn't in the house when Frannie bought it."

McCall shook her head. "In the wall we found newspapers she must have used to wipe up the blood. The dates on the papers bear out the fact that she was the owner of the house when the body went into the wall about twenty years ago. Frannie had to have known— even if she didn't personally put the body in the space and wall it up."

Rand had been standing, but now he pulled up a chair and sat down. "I knew Frannie Clementine most of my life. She went to our church. Hell, we had her over to dinner." He met her gaze. "I don't believe it. What did the granddaughter say?"

"She seemed to be in shock. I'm sure what we found took her by surprise, but I am curious what made them open the wall."

"Them?"

"Dawson Rogers was with her. He told me his puppy sensed something about the wall that scared her. There was a definite smell. Also, when Annabelle was getting the house ready to sell, she realized that an alcove had been walled over. I think they were just curious."

"How could Frannie have kept something like this a secret for...?"

"I don't think there would have been a smell since the

body was wrapped in multiple plastic sheeting, trussed up like a turkey, but the plastic had rotted and the some of the contents had leaked out."

Rand cringed. "And the Gilbert woman?" he asked, as if anxious to change the subject.

"Apparent accident."

The county attorney eyed her questioningly.

McCall shook her head. She didn't want to admit that she had a feeling it hadn't been a sad mishap. Inez had been wearing a coat and boots, as if she'd been outside. Also, deputies hadn't been able to locate the old woman's shotgun. McCall knew for a fact that she kept it by the front door. Inez had bragged about it, saying she liked to have it handy. Now it was missing.

DAWSON WOKE WORRIED about Annie. He got up to find the guest room empty. He found her sitting at the computer in his office. She looked up, startled to see him in the doorway.

"I didn't think you'd mind," she said.

He shook his head. "What are you looking at in the middle of the night?"

"The sheriff, when she called earlier, asked me if I'd ever heard of a man named Michael 'Mickey' Frazer."

Dawson stepped into the room and sat down on the edge of his desk. "Is that who was in the wall?"

She nodded. "McCall had found out the Marco Polo Heist and that Mickey worked for Bernie McDougal. What she doesn't know is the connection between Frannie and Bernie. Without the photos…" She broke down. "Isn't it bad enough that everyone will know Frannie was a murderer? Do they have to know that she was a mobster's moll?"

"Annie." He wanted desperately to comfort her but he was trying to keep his distance. Making love the other night had been a mistake—at least, he could tell she thought so. He knew better than to let it happen again—for his own heart's sake if not hers.

"Worse, I don't understand is how deep my grandmother is involved in all this," she said between sobs. "She had to be the one who killed that man and put him in the alcove and then walled it up. Along with jewels taken in the Marco Polo Heist there was a whole lot of cash. Apparently the museum hadn't taken the deposit to the bank. Because the Marco Polo exhibit had been so popular, there were thousands of dollars in a safe that was blown open. And I thought my grandmother lived all those years on my grandfather's insurance policy."

"Annie, you can't let this—"

"She must have been in on the heist. She was definitely in New York City at the time. Robbery is nothing compared to murder and hiding a body in your house behind a wall."

Dawson reached over and shut off the computer. "Come on, it's almost daylight. Let's get out of here." She let him pull her to her feet. "Get changed. I'll saddle up the horses."

THE SUN ROSE fiery red over the prairie. Annabelle breathed in the sweet scents of the late-fall day. She could see her breath in the cold morning air, but it felt good to be on a horse again. Good to get away from her troubles for a while.

She looked over at Dawson. Now, there was someone who felt at home in the saddle, she thought. Past him the Little Rockies loomed up into a brilliant blue sky. The breeze carried the scent of the pines as well as the creek next to them. Only a few golden leaves still remained on the cottonwoods. Fall here had always been a beautiful time. She realized how much she'd missed the seasons, missed a lot about Montana.

Her gaze went to Dawson again. Her heart ached. She was surprised by how much she'd missed him. Her life in California had been filled with busy, long, stress-filled days trying to make something of herself. She'd forgotten what it was like to just relax and enjoy the day.

"Better?" Dawson said.

She nodded and looked away, realizing she'd been staring at him. He'd aged wonderfully. If anything, he was more handsome. There was a confidence to him that had also grown. Dawson Rogers knew who he was, what he wanted, what tomorrow would bring and he was good with that.

Tears burned her eyes; she turned to swipe at them.

"It's going to be all right," he said softly as he rode beside her. "Once the sheriff is finished at the house, I'll go in and make that kitchen like new. You'll get the house sold and—"

"Dawson," she said, her voice breaking as she turned toward him. "I don't care about the house, about any of that."

He swung off his horse. The next thing she knew his

big hands were on her waist and he was lifting her down and into his arms. She let the tears come again, crying her heart out, soaking his jean jacket with her tears.

One hand smoothed her hair, while the other held her tightly to him. He said soothing words, whispered into her hair as he let her cry.

When she finally was able to stop, he handed her his bandanna. She wiped her eyes and blew her nose. He took the bandanna back, stuffing it into his pocket. She couldn't help but smile at him. He'd always been there for her. Always.

"I love you." The words came out on their own accord. She couldn't have stopped them even if she had wanted to. "I love you so much."

He nodded. "I love you, too." His voice sounded rough with emotion.

"The other day after we made love—"

"You don't have to explain," he said. "I know."

"You do?"

"We both got lost in the moment. I'm not sorry, but I know that it didn't change anything."

Hadn't it?

"Come on. Let's head back. I suspect the sheriff will be calling."

She looked into his face. There was so much she wanted to say to him. "I need to tell you—"

"You don't have to say it," he said, handing her the reins to her horse. "I know you appreciate my help. That's what old friends are for."

She took the reins, feeling her heart breaking all over again. She realized he wouldn't trust anything she said at this point. She'd just had her second emotional break-down. Given what had been found in her grandmother's kitchen wall, of course, she would be emotional.

But it was Dawson, being back here with him, that was killing her. She hadn't known what she wanted, but looking at him right now, he was all she wanted.

"Is there someone else?" she asked as he gave her a boost up into her saddle.

He seemed to hesitate for a moment. "I've been see-ing Amy Baker," he said, swinging up into his saddle. He reined his horse around. The sun had come up mak-ing the day shine. "That sun sure feels good, doesn't it? I'll make us some breakfast when we get back. You still love French toast?"

DAWSON HAD NEVER thought of himself as a coward, but he'd had to cut Annie off from whatever she was going to tell him. He couldn't bear the thought of her telling him that their lovemaking hadn't meant anything. That she was still heading back to her life in California once the house was sold.

Those were all things he already knew on an intel-lectual level, but he'd let his heart hope for a different outcome. Sometimes the way she looked at him, he would swear... But he knew that she'd been through so much, she probably didn't even know what she needed. He didn't want her making the wrong decision. But he didn't want her staying with him for the wrong reasons, either. He honestly didn't know what was right for her and he doubted she did either right now.

Back at the ranch, he'd sent her inside while he unsaddled their horses. Holding her earlier had made him want to throw down one of the horse blankets and make love to her out there in the wild. He wanted her so badly...

He pushed that thought as far back into his heart as he could. Once her house was sold... It was the mantra that kept playing in his head. But when he thought about her leaving, it almost knocked him to his knees.

"There you are."

He turned at the sound of his mother's voice.

"Are you all right?" she asked, closing the distance between them to look into his face as if she could read him like a child's book. "Oh, Dawson."

He shook his head, swallowing the lump in his throat. "I'll be fine."

She shook her head. "I heard what happened at the house. Annabelle's staying with you?" Her gaze searched his face.

"It isn't what you think. She's staying in the guest room." He'd never seen his mother cry, but right now she looked close to tears. He put his arm around her. "Once the sheriff lets her back into the house, I'll go over and get the kitchen fixed and then the house should be able to go on the market."

Her mother was shaking her head. "Who's going to buy it knowing..."

He'd thought of that and was sure Annabelle had, too. "I might have to buy it."

Willie nodded. "Okay, son. You could use it as a rental, I suppose. You're that anxious to get her on her way?"

"I have no choice."

"I suppose not." She sounded as sad about that as he did.

ANNABELLE HAD SEEN Willie drive up and head out to where Dawson was unsaddling the horses. She watched them for a moment before stepping into the bathroom to check herself in the mirror. Her cheeks were still pink from the November air. Her eyes weren't as bad as she thought they would be considering all the crying she'd done earlier. She couldn't help being embarrassed. Dawson, as usual, had been kind and understanding. It was his tenderness that kept breaking her heart.

Her cell phone rang. She stared down at the number. Clarisa? It was one of the models she used to work with. Her phone rang again. She thought about not answering it. She'd spoken to hardly anyone she'd worked with since everything went south. Clarisa was one of the new, younger models, but a sweet girl who was just starting in the business.

The phone rang again. Curiosity made her take the call. "Hello?"

"Annabelle, I'm so glad I got you. I was worried you wouldn't pick up. So, have you heard?"

Apparently not. "Heard what?"

"About Chambers. More models have come forward after hearing what happened to you. At first, everyone was scared to speak up, but then they did, one after another." Clarisa was laughing. "Chambers was arrested yesterday on assault charges. Everyone is talking about it. It happened because of you."

She couldn't believe what she was hearing. When she'd reported Gordon Chambers, she hadn't been believed. Gordon owned the top modeling agency in Southern California. If you crossed Gordon, your career was over. Annabelle had dodged his advances until he'd offered her a modeling job she would have given her eyeteeth for—but not at the cost of sleeping with him.

She'd told him what he could do with his job and then gone to the authorities, for all the good it had done. Chambers had instantly blackballed her. Word went out. She'd known he could hurt her. She hadn't realized how badly. He was telling everyone that she was impossible to work with and denying her charges. That's all it took and she couldn't get another job.

"I have even more good news," Clarisa was saying. "I ran into Thomas Darrington the other day. He asked if I'd seen you. Apparently he'd heard about Gordon blackballing you. Anyway, I brought him up to speed. He said he wants you for a big spread he's going to be doing after the first of the year. Girl, I really think you can have just about any job you want now. A lot of people had the same problem with Gordon and you brought him down."

Only she hadn't brought him down. She'd only started the ball rolling. She took a breath and let it out. Her heart was pounding. She could go back. She had a job. She'd always liked working with Thomas Darrington, an up-and-comer in the business and some-one she'd worked with before. Thomas had made her an offer she couldn't refuse. She could have her old life back. According to Clarisa, it was waiting for her.

"You need to take down Thomas's number and give him a call," her friend was saying. "He's really anxious to talk to you."

She found a notepad on Dawson's desk and wrote down the number. "Thank you for letting me know."

"I was afraid you hadn't heard," Clarisa said. "You were always so nice to me when some of those other models..." She laughed. "I hope you come back. Give me a call anytime. Also, I know a model who's looking for a roommate, if you're interested."

Annabelle disconnected and looked down at the number she'd written on the notepad. Next to it, she'd written *Thomas. Modeling job.* She still couldn't believe it. Just when she was at her lowest.

At the sound of Dawson's voice, she stuffed the note into her jeans pocket. As happy as she'd been just moments ago, she felt that awful pull on her heart. Could she really go back and leave here? Leave Dawson?

"Annabelle?"

Just the sound of his voice made her close her eyes for a moment, as if memorizing it. She loved him. He was all Montana cowboy. He'd never leave here. If she left him again, there would be no coming back.

# Chapter Eighteen

Dawson noticed the change in Annabelle when he and his mother entered the house. They'd all congregated in the kitchen, with Willie talking about how it wouldn't take long to get the house back in order and on the market.

Annabelle was quiet, nodding, but saying little. When their eyes met, he saw pain in them. There seemed to be a sadness to her, a resignation. He told himself he was glad he'd stopped her when they were out on horseback. More than ever, he felt that she'd been about to tell him what he already knew. That she was leaving as soon as the house sold.

He whipped up French toast, talking his mother into staying and joining them. He didn't want to be alone with Annabelle. He told himself that if he kept busy...

They'd turned the conversation to the weather and the upcoming holidays when Annabelle's cell phone rang. She pulled it out and glanced at the screen as if she'd been expecting a call. At her frown, he surmised that it wasn't the one she'd been waiting for.

Excusing herself, she stepped away from the table.

He and his mother both pretended not to listen, but it was clearly the sheriff calling to say they were finished at the house and she could move back in.

"You'll get the work done for her?" Willie asked.

He nodded as Annabelle returned to the table.

"Honey, you dropped something." His mother knelt to pick up what appeared to be a sheet from his office notepad. She glanced at the writing on it before handing it to Annabelle. Dawson couldn't miss what was written there. If he'd had any doubts, any hopes, they were dashed.

He watched Annabelle stuff the note into her pocket quickly. Her gaze locked with his for a moment and she seemed about to say something when Willie spoke.

"Dawson and I were just discussing your kitchen," his mother said. "Are we going to close off the alcove again or open it up?"

"You have both already done so much," Annabelle said.

"We finish what we start, isn't that right, Dawson?"

He was still looking into Annie's blue eyes, feeling his heart breaking all over again. He mentally cursed himself for letting it happen. Of course he'd fallen for her again. Hell, he'd never stopped loving her.

"I'll get right on it. The sooner the better," he said and got up to clear away the dishes.

"Let me help you with those," Annabelle said, but he quickly cut her off.

"I've got them."

"Yes," his mother said, as if seeing that he needed to be alone. "Annabelle, why don't you and I go back to the house and see what we need to pick up?"

Annabelle started to say something, but he heard his mother whisper, "Let's leave Dawson alone for a while, okay?"

ANNABELLE STARED AT Dawson's back. He'd seen the note. So had his mother. She wanted to tell him that she was torn, that she didn't know what she wanted, that she couldn't bear leaving him again. But she couldn't do that to him again. She'd put him through enough, so she left with Willie.

For much of the way into Whitehorse, neither of them spoke.

"Want to talk about it?" Willie finally asked.

"You saw that I've been offered a modeling job back in California. I'll admit that at first I was excited. I thought for sure I'd never get to work again."

"So it's good news."

She looked over at the older woman. "I can go back to that life. In fact, they want me back." She told Willie why she'd left and what had apparently happened.

"I'm so sorry," Willie said. "That must have been awful."

"Yes, it was. But the others came forward. They backed me up."

"So there is no reason you can't go back to the life you had."

"You know there is a reason," Annabelle said. "Just the thought of leaving Dawson again…" She had to look away as tears welled in her eyes. Determined not to break down again, she said. "I don't think I can leave him."

Willie looked over at her as they pulled up in front of the house behind Annabelle's car. "You love him."

"With all my heart. I always have. But I wanted to see what I could do outside of Whitehorse."

"What do you want now?" Willie asked, but before she could answer there was a tap on the window.

They both turned to see Mary Sue standing there as if waiting for them. Willie hesitated a moment, as if not wanting to quit their conversation, before she turned to put down her window.

Annabelle felt a moment of relief. What did she want to do?

"I thought you might need me," Mary Sue was saying. "The sheriff called me to say that the house was open. I suppose we'd better see how bad it is and decide what to do."

Willie agreed and put up her window. As Annabelle started to get out, the older woman touched her sleeve. "You know how I feel about you and about my son. Make the right decision for yourself. If you stay for the wrong reasons, you'll resent him and the life he has to offer you." She dropped her hand, smiling sadly. "I just want you both to be happy."

DAWSON HAD NO idea how much work undoing Frannie's remodeling in the kitchen would take. All he knew was that he had to do it quickly and then hope the house sold. If not, he would buy it. He'd already made up his mind. He would just have to do it through a subsidiary of the ranch corporation so Annabelle didn't know it was him buying it.

He wasn't far behind his mother. In fact, he drove up right as Annabelle was opening the house. Mary Sue was here, no doubt to see how bad it was going to be. That, or morbid curiosity. He imagined that would be the case for a lot of people once the house was on the market. Another reason he had to act quickly and probably buy the place. He didn't want Annie to have to go through that.

She opened the door and he saw her grimace. There was a definite smell. They all trailed inside. He pushed his way through, wanting to see how bad the kitchen was, to spare Annabelle if it was as bad as he suspected.

But she wasn't having any of that. She was right behind him. The alcove was wide open. The sheriff's department had made the opening larger to get the body out. It appeared that McCall had had someone clean up the floor. But the frame of the stained wall was still there. That was the first thing that would have to go.

He turned to find Annabelle staring at the hole. "Want it walled back up or opened?" he asked.

"Open. But I can't ask you to—"

"You aren't asking. I'm going to get my tools, tear the rest of this out, take up the floorboards. The flooring in the kitchen will have to be replaced but there isn't that much. It won't take long. I was thinking a nice hardwood floor." Before she could object because of the price, he added, "It will help sell the house, trust me."

She closed her mouth and nodded. "I do trust you. I already owe you so much."

"I'm sure money won't be a problem once you're back at work."

ANNABELLE DIDN'T GET a chance to reply as Mary Sue and Willie came into the kitchen. Mary Sue was complimenting everything that had been done. Willie offered to show her the rest of the house. The two of them left as Dawson headed for his pickup and tools.

She stood in the kitchen feeling almost dizzy. So much had happened. The poor old woman next door had died after falling down her stairs. Not to mention Annabelle's grandmother had walled up a man in her kitchen.

"Is there anything I can—"

Dawson cut her off as he returned with his tools. "I've got it. I called for the subfloor sheeting and the lumber to be delivered. This won't take long."

She nodded and stepped out of his way as he strapped on his tool belt. He couldn't have looked more sexy, she thought and quickly moved out of his way.

From upstairs came voices. Willie and Mary Sue were visiting, discussing people they both knew. It seemed most people in Whitehorse were related to each other in some way.

Annabelle walked down to her bedroom. It was the last room of the house to be painted and cleaned out. She closed the door and called Chloe. "Hi," she said when her sister answered.

"What's wrong?"

She let out a nervous laugh. "You can tell by that one word?"

"I know you, remember?"

Yes, unfortunately, her sisters did know her. That's why they didn't like her. "Something's happened." She explained about the walled-up alcove and what had been found inside.

"You can't be serious. A man's body?"

"I'm afraid so. Would you let TJ know? From what the sheriff has told me, it's been in there for years. I remembered there used to be an alcove there. Do you remember it?"

"I suppose. It's just been so long. I'm not sure I would have remembered. You're saying this happened when?"

"After we all left home. That's what the coroner thinks so somewhere in the past thirteen years."

"How did he get into the wall?" Chloe asked.

Annabelle stifled a laugh. The question was so like her sister. *Oh, he just crawled into the alcove and curled up to die while Grandma built a wall around him.* "He was murdered, wrapped in plastic and walled up in the kitchen."

"They can't think Grandmother did that!" her sister cried.

"I'm afraid that's exactly what they think." Annabelle thought of the photos and the newspaper clippings. It was all going to come out. She figured warning her sisters was the kindest thing she could do.

She told Chloe about what she'd found under the floorboard and under her bed, along with what she found in the metal box.

"That is the most ridiculous thing I have ever heard," Chloe snapped when she was finished. "Our grandmother was not a mobster's girlfriend."

"The dead man worked for the mobster. The sheriff thinks the man followed Grandma from New York and that the reason she killed him probably has to do with the Marco Polo Heist, a famous robbery back in New York. They've never found the jewels or the money that was taken."

Chloe had fallen silent.

"I'm sorry to hit you with all of this, but it is going to come out," Annabelle said.

"What is that noise?"

"Dawson is in the kitchen removing the rest of the wall and putting down new flooring."

"That house is never going to sell."

Annabelle thought her sister was probably right about that. Murder houses weren't that popular. "I will probably be returning to California and keeping the house on the market. I've been offered a really good modeling job." Annabelle glanced in the direction of the kitchen. "Unless I decide to stay."

"You're thinking about staying? You have to stay at least until Christmas. TJ and I have already bought our tickets. We were going to surprise you. Surprise! We're coming up there to help you sell the house and have Christmas together. We were planning to be there a few days before Christmas Eve."

"Really?"

"Would that be all right or do you need to get to your job before then?"

"No, it would be wonderful." Annabelle was having trouble believing they really were coming back to help her so the three of them could have Christmas together, especially after she'd just told them the news.

"Now, more than ever, I feel like we should be together for the holidays," Chloe said.

Annabelle was fighting tears when she heard the knock at her bedroom door. "I couldn't be happier," she said, her voice breaking. "I have to go, but I will talk to you soon."

"Am I interrupting?" Willie asked when Annabelle opened the door, still fighting tears.

She shook her head. "That was my sister Chloe. She and TJ are coming up to spend Christmas with me."

"That's wonderful." Willie hugged Annabelle. "I'm happy for you." As she pulled back, she said, "Dawson thought things would go faster if you came out to the house and stayed at the ranch until he's finished."

She could see what the two of them were trying to do. "Thank you, but I'm staying here."

"Are you sure?" Willie asked, glancing over her shoulder toward the kitchen.

"I'm sure." Annabelle smiled. "My grandmother left me this house because she knew I was the one who could deal with all this."

"Yes, you're plenty strong," Dawson's mother agreed.

He called from the kitchen, wanting Annabelle to see if she liked the hardwood floor he'd ordered.

"I'm going to take off, then," Willie said. "If you change your mind…"

"I know where you live," Annabelle said with a smile. "Thank you again for everything."

"You bet," Willie said and called goodbye to her son as she left.

Dawson looked surprised. "I thought she was going to ask you to stay at the ranch."

"She did. I'm staying here."

He didn't look happy to hear that. "It's going to be noisy and dusty."

"I'll make do. My sisters are coming up for Christmas." She laughed at his surprise.

"So you're staying that long? What about the job offer?"

"It wouldn't start until after the holidays. But I'm not sure I'm going to take it, anyway. I still have to get the house sold."

"Maybe you'll get lucky and the house will sell and there won't be anything keeping you here after the holidays," he said and turned away to show her the flooring.

"It's beautiful. Thank you. I'm getting better at accepting help, don't you think?"

He glanced over at her. "You are."

"Who says people can't change?" With that, she turned and left him to it.

ROB COULDN'T BELIEVE how quickly the house had filled up again after the sheriff's department finished its investigation. He'd kept his ear to the ground, but it seemed there hadn't been anything else of interest found.

"I think the old girl got rid of the loot," he grumbled to himself. "Maybe she didn't even try to fence it. Could have sold it to a private collector. It wasn't like she hadn't met the kind of people who would have been interested. And now my uncle thinks she did him a favor? The foolish old coot definitely has dementia."

Still, he knew what his uncle would have said. Someone would have talked if they'd bought the gems. That was the problem with even the filthy rich, they liked to brag. If one of them had bought the jewels from Francesca Clementine, word would have gotten back to Bernie. And the old gal would have died a long time ago.

So she'd kept it for whatever reason. Hidden them like she had poor Mickey's body. He cringed at the thought of being walled up in a house like that. Sure, the goon was dead, but still.

Frannie, as everyone referred to her, had stiffed Bernie, gotten out of town and come out West telling everyone she was a widow. The woman probably couldn't have told the truth if her life depended on it. She couldn't have found a husband, gotten knocked up and become a widow that quickly, unless...

He frowned. Not long after arriving, she'd bought the house and given birth to a son, according to the local gossips he'd overhead at the café downstairs in the hotel. As far as anyone knew, she'd never had a full-time job other than raising her grandkids when they'd come to live with her when they were young. His frown deepened.

He stopped pacing to count on his fingers, then swore.

His uncle had wondered for over fifty years why she'd left like she had. He counted again to make sure before he picked up the phone. "You aren't going to like this," he said and then told Bernie. Let him do the math.

"I'M CALLING IT a day," Dawson said as he put away his tools. He'd looked up to find Annabelle standing in the doorway.

"I can't believe how much you got done," she said. "It looks great. I like that that stupid wall isn't still there."

"You sure you aren't going to have nightmares tonight?" he asked seriously as he closed his toolbox and straightened.

"No," she said, realizing it was true. "It's funny, but this house seemed more creepy with that wall. Now that's it's gone and what was behind it, I'm fine." She shook her head. "At least I know now why my grandmother left the house to me." She had to smile. "She said I was a lot like her."

"I hope not," Dawson said with a laugh.

"I guess we'll never know for sure what happened here. If McCall is right, then it all has to do with that museum exhibit on Marco Polo and the stolen jewels. I'd like to think the man's death was self-defense—and that grandmother did what she had to do to protect us all. If she was running from her mobster boyfriend… We already know that she was pregnant, probably with his child. It's funny. She always seemed so…content, as if she'd made her peace with the past and everything else."

"She did a good job of raising you girls and everyone in this community loved her."

"Well, they *did*. Wait until they learn about the man she kept in her wall."

"This town is pretty forgiving. Your grandmother did so much good in this community. That's what will be remembered."

"I hope so."

He stood for moment just looking at her. She felt the chemistry sparking between them and a whole lot of good past history making the kitchen suddenly seem too warm. "I should get goin'."

Annabelle stepped out of his way and let him walk out. She was staying for Christmas. There would be time to see how he felt about her maybe staying around. She watched him drive away and then closed the door and locked it.


"I WASN'T SURE you'd be back to the ranch tonight," Willie said as Dawson walked into her kitchen to find her standing over the stove.

"I don't know why not," he said and leaned in to see what she was busy stirring. "Chili?"

She nodded. "The way you and your brother like it."

"I thought we'd be eating leftover turkey for a few weeks," he said as he leaned against the counter to watch. When his mother was fretting over something, she cooked. He didn't have to ask what was bothering her.

"That huge old turkey carcass got picked clean at Thanksgiving," Willie said. "That's what's nice about having a lot of people over. Not a lot of leftovers."

"You don't mind me using some of the ranch funds to buy Annabelle's house?"

"I think it's a good investment."

He wasn't so sure about that. "I figure the sale will go through pretty quickly so she should be able to leave right after the holidays."

"Sounds like you have it all worked out." Willie stopped stirring the chili to turn to face him. With a sigh, she said, "I'm worried about you."

"I'll be fine."

"She doesn't want to go." Willie made it sound as if it was hard for her to tell him that.

"What would make you think that?"

His mother gave him a look. "You live as long as I have and you know things. She just doesn't know how to tell you so neither of you think she's taking the easy way out."

He shook his head. "Don't take this wrong, but this time, you're wrong." He started to turn away but she caught his arm and pulled him back.

"I was thinking as I was making this chili. Maybe it's time for some sort of grand gesture, you know, like they do in movies, to let her know how you feel."

Dawson chuckled at that. "She knows how I feel, Mama." He hadn't called her that since he was a boy.

She let go of his arm. "You want some chili?"

"I'm not hungry, but thanks." With that he left and headed to his own home, knowing that without Annie there it would feel empty—just like he felt.

ANNABELLE WOKE WITH a start. For a moment, she thought the sound had come from under the bed, but Dawson had secured the trapdoor with the nails. No one was coming up through that door.

She lay in bed listening. There was a strange light coming through the curtains. She frowned and quietly climbed out of bed to look. After a longer than normal Indian summer, winter had come while she was sleeping.

The first blizzard of the season had blown in. She could tell that the temperature had dropped drastically from the ice that was forming on the inside of the old windows. The sky, which should have been dark, was a pale gray color as huge snowflakes whirled in the wind, sticking to anything they touched.

She shivered and climbed back into bed, telling herself she must have heard the wind. Gripping the covers under her chin, she lay still, listening to the wind—until she heard a sound that sent her pulse into overdrive. The front door had just blown open!

ROB HAD KNOWN his uncle was going to be furious.

"She was pregnant? Pregnant with my kid?"

"If you do the math—"

"I did the math. I had a son I knew nothing about? Where is he now?"

"Died in a car wreck with his wife when the youngest kid was, like, four or five, I heard. You can't believe the way people talk in these small towns. If you stay here long enough, you hear—"

"So that's my grandkid staying at the house," his uncle said, clearly not listening to him. "My granddaughter. And Baby Doll kept this all from me." He was swearing again.

"So, what do you want me to do?"

"What I told you to do. Find the damned loot. But don't touch a hair on my granddaughter's head. You got that?"

He couldn't believe the old man was getting senti-mental in his old age.

"I got it. But what do I do if she catches me in the house?"

"Figure it out. But don't you hurt her. Not one hair."

He'd hung up doing some cussing of his own. Then he'd gotten dressed and started to leave the motel, only to find that a snowstorm had blown in. Just his luck. But he couldn't put this off any longer. He would break into the house and finish his search. If he was right, no way would the granddaughter be staying in the house—not after a body had been hauled out of it.

ANNABELLE SCRAMBLED OUT of bed and rushed into the living room to close the front door. She turned on a light and was about to bolt the door, when she heard a noise behind her. Turning quickly, she saw the snowy foot-prints melting on the floor a second before she came face-to-face with Lawrence Clarkston, the old man with the cane who'd sworn he was Frannie's beau. He'd lied, according to Inez. Worse, she'd noticed his car parked in front of the neighbor woman's house across the street.

She stared at him, shocked to see him standing in the empty living room. Even more surprised to see the gun in his hand. He motioned for her to step away from the door.

"Where's the jewels?" he demanded. "I know your grandmother still had them when she died. She might have spent the money, but she still had the gems."

Annabelle groaned. "I don't know anything about any jewels."

"My brother followed your mother out here. I never knew where he ended up. She'd changed her name, her looks, everything. I'm amazed Mickey was even able to get a lead on her. Bernie was losing his mind trying to find her. He's been looking for her for years. My brother finds her and she kills him!"

She didn't know what to say. "If you knew your brother found her—"

"He called, told me he'd found her but didn't give me any specifics. Damned fool. He thought he could keep the jewels for him, fence them and not have Bernie find out. I was trying to talk him out of it, telling him how dangerous it would be." He laughed. "Instead, Bernie's Baby Doll kills him?"

"He must have told you something since you showed up at my door days before the body was found," Annabelle said. She didn't know who or what to believe. This old man had lied to her once already.

"I've kept my ear to the ground for years. When I heard where Bernie was living now, I made sure I got a room down the hall. He doesn't know me from Adam, but I know him. He corrupted my brother. Mickey was a good guy before he met Bernie."

"So Bernie knows about Frannie?"

He nodded. "You know why they called him Bernie the Hawk? 'Cuz he had an eye for the ladies—until your grandmother came along. He fell so hard for that woman. My brother said anyone could have told him she was trouble, but no one had the guts. I laughed my ass off when I heard that she stole it all and disappeared."

Her mind was racing. She glanced around for a way

out. Since they'd pretty much cleaned out the house, there was no handy weapon. The door was a few steps behind her, but she doubted she could turn and reach it before the man shot her.

"Look," he was saying. "Mickey wasn't all that bright. I thought he'd taken off with the jewels. But when I happened to see the newspaper in Bernie's trash at the rest home, I got curious. Bernie was all excited. Everyone at the home was talking about it. I went online, saw the Milk River Courier newspaper and checked out what Bernie had cut from it. The moment I saw your grandmother's face…" He smiled. "Bernie must have felt the same thing. Your grandmother was a looker. Played Bernie like a Stradivarius. Did you know she never told him her real name? He just called her Baby Doll."

The old man took a breath. "When I found out that Bernie had sent his worthless nephew, Robby, out here, I thought it was going to be another wild-goose chase. How wrong I was. So hand over the jewels and I'm out of here."

She started to tell him again that she really didn't know anything, when they both jumped at the sound of glass breaking.

Lawrence swore and said, "Stay right here." The moment he started toward her bedroom, she quickly unlocked the door. She didn't think the old man could move fast enough to catch her and once she was outside in the blizzard—

Annabelle had the door open and was almost outside when she slammed into a dark figure that appeared out of nowhere. She realized he must have thrown something at her bedroom window to distract the old man. This man wasn't old. He was big and strong and he literally lifted her up by her shoulders and thrust her back inside the house. He'd just slammed the door behind him when Lawrence came running into the room, gun firing.

The younger man pushed her out of the way and drew his own weapon, firing at the approaching target. The old man staggered and went down. "Larry the Loser? What the hell is he doing here?"

She watched in horror as the younger man walked over and picked up the gun the old man had dropped. He pocketed it. Everything had happened so fast that she hadn't even moved. Now, as she started to bolt for the door, he turned to point his gun at her.

"Tell me you aren't going to give me as much trouble as your grandmother did my uncle," the man said.

"Your uncle?" she managed to get out. This must be Robby, the guy old man had mentioned.

"Bernie. He said to say hello. You realize he's your grandfather, right?"

Annabelle felt as if she'd fallen down a rabbit hole. "Yes, my grandfather."

"So, just give me whatever is left that she took from my uncle and I'm out of your hair, so to speak."

She groaned. "I just told that man I don't know anything about any loot."

"You threw a lot of stuff away. You're sure you didn't come across some jewels? Rubies, pearls, diamonds, emeralds?"

"My grandmother didn't have anything like that. She

didn't wear jewelry, so she didn't even have costume jewelry."

"Didn't wear jewelry?" He scoffed at that. "My uncle weighed down that woman with diamond necklaces and earrings. On her birthday, he gave her an emerald ring that set him back a small fortune. You're telling me she got rid of all of his gifts?"

"Apparently. I suspect that's how she lived as long as she did. I never saw any jewelry, ever." She took a step closer to the door.

He waved her back with the gun in his hand and a shake of his head. "We're still talking here."

MAKE A GRAND GESTURE. Dawson couldn't get the phrase out of his head. What exactly did his mother expect him to do? Show up like he had the last time, with an engagement ring and a bouquet of roses—both things he couldn't afford. That had been his grand gesture and look where it had gotten him.

No, he was fresh out of grand gestures. But as he drove through the blizzard toward home, he couldn't get Annabelle off his mind. He hadn't liked leaving her in that house alone.

He wasn't concerned with ghosts. He didn't think she would be, either. She was a strong woman and she was handling all of this remarkably well.

Still, when he reached the turn-off to his house, he kept going in the direction of town. He told himself it wouldn't hurt to drive by her place. It was late, since, after talking to his mother, he'd gone out to the barn and worked on his old tractor for a while. It had seemed a symbolic thing to do. Also the damned thing wasn't running again.

The snowstorm roared around him making it difficult to see where the road started and ended. He felt the need to drive faster, to get there quicker, and told himself he was letting his imagination run away with him. Maybe he was more spooked by what they'd found at the house than Annie was. Annie. He did much better when he thought of her as Annabelle.

Through the falling, whirling snow, he caught a glimpse of the lights of Whitehorse. He told himself she'd be in bed, sound asleep, not having given a thought to him.

But still, he sped up a little on the outskirts of town. It wasn't far now.

ROB STUDIED HER. He thought she was telling the truth. He'd been hanging around long enough to know that this woman had been some kind of supermodel until she fell on hard times and came back here to sell her grandmother's house. He'd even heard that her fancy sports car out in the yard was almost repossessed for lack of payment. Someone at the local bar had seen Dawson Rogers write the repo man a check. The car had already been hooked up to the wrecker. A few more minutes and it would have been gone.

"Look, I need to call my uncle with this news. He won't be happy. Normally he would tell me to torture you until you told me the truth. But the fact that you are his flesh and blood and Baby Doll's granddaughter,

I think he'll cut you some slack. You have to be honest with me, though, okay?"

Her mind had been racing. "You found the tunnel," she said as she was putting things together. "I would imagine you already looked down there and in the garage. I don't know of any more hiding places. I never knew any of this about my grandmother. It all came as a shock, including the dead man in the wall."

Rob was considering that when he heard a sound behind him. He spun, just not quickly enough. For a moment, he couldn't figure out what had hit him. But glancing over his shoulder, he saw the sword blade sticking out of his back. When he looked at the old man he'd thought he killed, he saw that he was holding the shell of his cane.

Rob lifted the gun to fire, but as he turned, it felt as if someone had cut his strings. Before he could get a shot off, he slumped to the floor at the old man's feet. "Bernie isn't going to like this, Larry," he choked out before everything went black.

ANNABELLE WATCHED ALL of this play out before her eyes as if in a bad dream. It wasn't until the younger man slumped to the floor that she found her feet.

She made a run for the door, but the old man was faster than he looked even wounded. He grabbed a handful of hair and jerked her back. His rancid breath washed over her face as he pulled her close and whispered, "He might have believed you, but I'm betting you're going to tell me where the loot is before this night is over because I could care less if you're Bernie's granddaughter."

She could hear the storm raging outside. The old man jerked her hair harder, making her cry out in pain. She could see that he was bleeding, but clearly the gunshot wasn't going to kill him. Apparently he'd been listening to her conversation with Rob.

"Let's go in this room down here," Larry said. "Your bedroom. I saw through the window that it's about the only room with stuff still in it. Is that where the loot is?"

"I told you just like I told the other man. There is no jewelry."

"Right," the old man said, giving her a hard shove. "Maybe I can help jog your memory."

She stumbled into her room, banging against the closet door where her grandmother's clothing still hung. Her mind raced to think if there was something in here that she could use for a weapon. She spotted her hammer on the dresser.

Larry went to the closet. Keeping one eye on her, he began to tear Frannie's clothes from their hangers. One gawdy sweatshirt after another hit the floor.

Annabelle inched a little closer to the dresser and the hammer sitting on top. Larry saw her out of the corner of his eye and lunged at her, throwing her across the bed. He smacked her across the face, holding her down as he reached to grab the cord on the blinds. She tried to kick him in the groin only to have him slap her harder.

The cord snapped off and he roughly rolled her onto her face on the bed and began to tie her hands together behind her back.

"You're hurting me," she cried out.

"I've only just begun. You try anything and I'll kill you because, according to you, you know nothing, right? I can hog-tie you and I will if you move again."

She rolled to her side and watched him as he went back to the closet. He pulled down boxes of old shoes, throwing them onto the growing pile until the closet was empty.

He was breathing hard when he came back over to where she lay. "Okay, girlie, now we're going to get down to business." He pulled a knife from a scabbard under his pants leg. She tried to recoil, but he grabbed her hair again as he laid the edge of the blade against her cheek. "You were your grandmother's favorite, according to the woman across the street who I visited for a while recently. These little old ladies are so helpful. If Frannie confided in anyone, it would have been you. Tell me where it is!"

DAWSON SAW THE lights on Annie's bedroom and the living room the moment he pulled up. He couldn't explain what had him so afraid. Just a bad feeling. He rushed up to the house and pounded on the door. She would think he was crazy. Think he was butting into her life. Again. But he didn't care. He had to see her. Had to see if she was all right.

The light in the bedroom went out.

"Oh, no, you don't," he said as he pounded harder. "Annie, you might as well open up, because I'm not going anywhere until you do!" he yelled.

The light came back on in the bedroom. A few minutes later, the door opened a crack.

Annabelle's pale face peered out. "What do you want?" she demanded, her voice cracking.

He noticed there was a red mark on the side of her face. Had she been asleep?

"You need to leave." Her blue eyes seemed to plead with him. "Please."

"I just had to be sure you were all right. I know it sounds crazy but... Could I come in for a moment?"

She shook her head. "No. Now, please go." She began to close the door.

As she was closing the door, his bad feeling was even stronger, now that he'd seen her. Before she could get the door all the way shut and locked, he slammed his hand into it, forcing her back so he could enter.

Bursting into the empty living room, he shoved to the side. As he turned, he found some old man holding a gun to Annie's temple.

"Close the door," the old man ordered. "Lock it. Play hero and she dies."

Off to the side, he could see a body with a sword sticking out of it. His throat constricted. He'd been right about Annie being in trouble. But now he might have made it worse.

ANNABELLE LET OUT a cry as the man jabbed the gun against her temple and twisted her arm behind her as he dragged her to him. He was much stronger and quicker than he looked.

"Close the door," Larry ordered. "Now!"

Dawson did as the man asked. "What's going on?" He sounded so calm.

"He thinks my grandmother had the jewels from the heist and that I know where they are," she said, her voice breaking. If only Dawson had just left like she'd asked him. She couldn't bear the thought that he was going to die because of her.

"That's ridiculous," Dawson snapped. "She didn't even know about the heist or her grandmother's relationship with Bernie McDougal."

"Or about my brother being murdered and walled up in her grandmother's house?" the old man said.

"I was the one who wanted to know what was behind that wall. Let her go. She doesn't know anything."

"Maybe. Maybe not. But unless you want to see her die, you'll do exactly what I say." Larry motioned with the gun for Dawson to go down the hall toward her bedroom.

She didn't believe for a moment that he would let them go when he didn't find anything. Or even if he did.

Dawson was ahead of them as they started toward the bedroom. She feared what would happen once they reached there. Larry still had her arm pulled behind her, but the gun was no longer to her head. She knew it was risky, but she saw no other way. "Dawson!" she called and spun around, even though it hurt her arm.

She kicked Larry as hard as she could in his private parts. As she did, she grabbed the gun. The old man doubled over, but his grip on the gun was still too strong for her to wrestle it from him. She feared he would get off a shot at Dawson before she could. From behind her, she heard the sound of Dawson's boots on the old hardwood floor as he rushed toward them. As he did, he pulled the sword from Robby's body.

He drove the blade into the man's side, forcing him back. Larry's grip on the gun gave. She jerked it from his hand as he stumbled back and dropped to the floor.

Dawson took the gun from her and held it on the man. It had all happened so fast. She felt dizzy, fear still coursing through her even with a sense of relief. Was it really over? Or would there be others who would come looking for the loot?

Trembling, she listened to Dawson make the call to the sheriff. Then he pulled her into his arms as they stood over the old man until they heard the sound of sirens. Moments later, deputies were streaming through the front door.

# Chapter Nineteen

Annabelle didn't know how long she'd been asleep when she felt something warm and wet touch her cheek. Her eyes flew open. She jerked back, a laugh escaping her lips as Dawson's puppy gave her another kiss.

"Sadie, no," he cried as he rushed into the room. "She has been wanting to come see you for hours. I thought I'd closed the door all the way after I checked on you earlier. How are you?"

"Good, thanks to you."

"Well, when you're ready, I made you something special for breakfast." With that, he called the puppy, who scampered out and the door closed.

Annabelle looked around for her clothes and groaned when she realized that last night she'd thrown on one of her grandmother's sweatshirts and her jeans. She pulled on the sweatshirt, thinking about her grandmother. Was she really like Frannie? Her grandmother had been a survivor. Annabelle guessed she could say that about herself too.

"Something smells good," she said as she walked into Dawson's kitchen.

"I thought you might be hungry. You slept a long time. It's almost noon."

She couldn't believe it. Then again, last night she remembered his arm around her all the way out to his house. He'd helped her inside and into the bed. She remembered trying to thank him, but he'd already closed the door. The next thing she knew, she was waking to Sadie's kisses.

"You saved my life last night," she said, her voice breaking. "If you hadn't come back to look in on me..."

"For once my instincts were right," he said and turned back to dishing up the Mexican quiche he'd made.

The smell of it brought back other memories of the two of them. Dawson had always been a great cook. There wasn't anything the man couldn't do.

"Your instincts weren't wrong thirteen years ago," she said as he put a slice in front of her along with a bowl of fresh fruit. "I wanted so badly to marry you. The ring, the roses..." Her voice broke again. "But I couldn't."

He nodded, his brown eyes serious. "I know. There were things you had to do. I was incredibly selfish asking you to give up your dream."

"I'm not going back to modeling. I know you said you're seeing Amy now, but—"

"Annie, you can't make a decision like that so soon after everything that's happened."

"I'm not going to change my mind. Also, I'm going to give Amy Baker a run for her money. I want you back, Dawson."

He shook his head. "Annie."

"My life was so up in the air the night we made love. But I'm perfectly clear on what I want now. I love you. I'll wait for you. I'll talk to Mary Sue about keeping the house and I think I can get a job down at the grocery store. If not there, then—"

He reached across the breakfast bar and took her face in his big hands. Bending, he kissed her. She forgot all about the quiche. All about everything except being in this man's arms again. She kissed him back as he swept her up and carried her to his bedroom.

They made love slowly until neither of them could stand it any longer. And then they let the chemistry burn between them in a fire that Annabelle knew would last the rest of their lives.

Later, lying naked in his arms, she looked up at him. He was her Montanan and she was finally home.

"When I said maybe you needed a grand gesture," Willie cried when they came in the kitchen door, "I didn't mean almost getting yourself killed." She rushed to her son, cupping his face in her hands and just looking at him, as if too thankful to speak.

"But I got the girl," he said and smiled.

"Oh, you boys are going to be the death of me," Willie said and stepped to Annabelle and hugged her tightly. "You're staying."

She nodded. "I'm not going anywhere." Dawson put his arm around her.

Willie smiled at them. "I'm so glad the two of you are all right."

"The nightmare is over," Dawson said.

"I wish that were true. It won't be over until the jewels from the heist turn up," Annabelle said. "We can't even be sure that my grandmother had them. Obviously, my grandfather still believes she does and so do his... associates. He believes she stole them when she took off without a word and disappeared. He's been looking for her and the loot for more than fifty years. I doubt he will stop now."

Willie shook her head, as if in wonder, and Annabelle realized she was staring at her ugly sweatshirt. "It was my grandmother's. She has a closet full of them."

"I bet she does," the older woman said. "I've never seen anything like it. I noticed you were wearing a clown one the other day. What is this one?"

"A unicorn," Annie said with a groan.

"May I?" Willie asked as she began to pry at one of the green stones that made up the ground the unicorn was standing on. "It's been a while since I've seen an emerald, but I'd swear this is one."

"What?" Dawson and Annie said in unison.

Willie handed the stone to her son. "I think we've found what happened to the missing jewels. Your grandmother knew there would be others coming to find them, so she hid them in broad daylight."

Dawson looked at Annie. "I think she's right. You say there are a dozen of these in her closet?"

Annabelle nodded in disbelief. "We need to call the sheriff."

"ARE YOU SURE you want to keep the house?" Dawson asked as he finished setting up the last of the furniture in the spare bedroom. Fortunately, they'd been able to retrieve a lot of it from the charity shop, assuring them it would only be temporary.

"My sisters are coming home for Christmas. I think we need to stay here. At least for the holidays. This is where we were raised."

"I was planning to buy the house, anyway," he confessed as he stepped to her to take her in his arms and kiss her.

"Aren't you tired of rescuing me yet?"

"No chance."

They both turned at a knock on the door. A deliveryman stood on the porch. When Annabelle opened the door, he asked her to sign for the large envelope he held in his hand. She signed, curious.

After he left, she stepped back inside and showed Dawson. "It's from Bernie in New York. Do I dare open it?" She looked at him and then laughed, thinking of the wall over the alcove. Her future husband was even more curious than she was.

She tore into it to find a letter-sized envelope inside with a note attached to it.

*I'm one of Bernie McDougal's nurses. He asked me to make sure you got this. It was his dying wish.*

She looked up at Dawson and slowly opened the letter.

My dear granddaughter,

I'm sorry I'll never get to meet you.

But I wanted you to know how much I loved your grandmother. Whatever she might have done, it was to protect the child she was carrying and later her three granddaughters.

My nephew told me that everyone said you were the one most like your grandmother. In that case, I know you must be beautiful and have her spunk. So I also know that you will do just fine.

I wish you well. You will be safe now,
Bernie, your grandfather

Annabelle had tears in her eyes as she refolded the letter. She looked at Dawson. "Aren't you worried that I might have inherited some of my grandparent's genes?"

He laughed and pulled her to him. "I can handle it."

She smiled up into his handsome face. "I know you can, cowboy."

Annabelle cuddled against Dawson. She'd come home and there was no other place on earth that she wanted to be.

Her sisters would be here soon. It was going to be a wonderful Christmas, she thought, as she looked around the house Dawson and his mother had helped her get ready for her family.

Outside the snow continued to fall. Nothing like a white Christmas, she thought.

She only had one wish. That her grandmother were here to share it with them. Then again, she thought with a smile, knowing Frannie the way she did now, she figured she was here in spirit.

\* \* \* \* \*

# Get 4 FREE REWARDS!

We'll send you 2 FREE Books **plus** 2 FREE Mystery Gifts.

**Harlequin® Intrigue** books feature heroes and heroines that confront and survive danger while finding themselves irresistibly drawn to one another.

FREE Value Over **$20**

**Chapter One**

The old antique Royal typewriter clacked with each angry stroke
of the keys. Shaking fingers pounded out livid words onto the old
discolored paper. As the fury built, the fingers moved faster and
faster until the keys all tangled together in a metal knot that lay
suspended over the paper.

With a curse of frustration, the metal arms were tugged apart
and the sound of the typewriter resumed in the small room. Angry
words burst across the page, some letters darker than others as the
keystrokes hit like a hammer. Other letters appeared lighter, some
dropping down a half line as the fingers slipped from the worn keys.
A bell sounded at the end of each line as the carriage was returned
with a clang, until the paper was ripped from the typewriter.

Read in a cold, dark rage, the paper was folded hurriedly, the
edges uneven, and stuffed into the envelope already addressed in
the black typewritten letters:

Author TJ St. Clair
Whitehorse, Montana

The stamp slapped on, the envelope sealed, the fingers still
shaking with expectation for when the novelist opened it. The

HIEXP0918

fan rose and smiled. Wouldn't Ms. St. Clair, aka Tessa Jane Clementine, love this one.

***

TJ St. Clair hated conference calls. Especially this conference call.

"I know it's tough with your book coming out before Christmas," said Rachel the marketing coordinator, her voice sounding hollow on speakerphone in TJ's small New York City apartment.

"But I don't have to tell you how important it is to do as much promo as you can this week to get those sales where you want them," Sherry from Publicity and Events added.

TJ held her head and said nothing for a moment. "I'm going home for the holidays to be with my sisters, who I haven't seen in months." She started to say she knew how important promoting her book was, but in truth she often questioned if a lot of the events really made that much difference—let alone all the social media. If readers spent as much time as TJ had to on social media, she questioned how they could have time to read books.

"It's the threatening letters you've been getting, isn't it?" her agent Clara said.

She glanced toward the window, hating to admit that the letters had more than spooked her. "That is definitely part of it. They have been getting more...detailed and more threatening."

"I'm so sorry, TJ," Clara said and everyone added in words of sympathy.

"You've spoken to the police?" her editor, Dan French, asked.

"There is nothing they can do until...until the fan acts on the threats. That's another reason I want to go to Montana."

For a few beats there was silence. "All right. I can speak to Marketing," Dan said. "We'll do what we can from this end."

*Don't miss*
**Rogue Gunslinger** *by B.J. Daniels,*
*available October 2018 wherever*
*Harlequin® Intrigue books and ebooks are sold.*

www.Harlequin.com

# *Love Harlequin romance?*

## DISCOVER.

Be the first to find out about promotions,
news and exclusive content!

Facebook.com/HarlequinBooks

Twitter.com/HarlequinBooks

Instagram.com/HarlequinBooks

Pinterest.com/HarlequinBooks

ReaderService.com

## EXPLORE.

Sign up for the Harlequin e-newsletter and
download a free book from any series at
**TryHarlequin.com.**

## CONNECT.

Join our Harlequin community to share
your thoughts and connect with other
romance readers!
**Facebook.com/groups/HarlequinConnection**

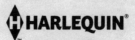

**ROMANCE WHEN
YOU NEED IT**

HSOCIAL2018